The Spice Hound's Adventures

Jerry Reid

Published by Oxbow Publishing, 2025.

This is a work of fiction. Similarities to real people, places, or events are entirely coincidental.

THE SPICE HOUND'S ADVENTURES

First edition. March 23, 2025.

Copyright © 2025 Jerry Reid.

ISBN: 979-8230436553

Written by Jerry Reid.

Table of Contents

This book is dedicated to my wife, friend, partner and cruising companion, Joni Reid.

Early on, when we first met, I was told "she always rises to the occasion." And she certainly has, whether it's navigating into a tricky anchorage on a storm-tossed night, cutting losses on a failed adventure, or editing our sea stories to make them more palatable.

I'm a lucky man.

The Spice Hound's Route on his Odyssey

Odessa, Texas	Short-order cook at a diner, Giselle
Dallas, Texas	On the road to Houston
Houston, Texas	Cook on the scrap metal freighter
Honduras	Finas Blankenship's ghosts
Panama Canal	Howler monkeys
Hawaii	Drop off cargo
Hong Kong	Engine trouble, buys motorcycle
Chinese villages	Elephant trial
Route to the Mekong	Tigers on the road
Mekong River	Lotu Chee, pirates, a fireship
Mekong Delta	Bull sharks
Singapore	Missing people, Deepavali festival
Langkawi	Max Chee, Lotu to school
Phuket	Justice
Jakarta	Route to Ambon
Ambon	Spices, at last
Buru Island	Brush with evil, reunion?

Southeast Asia Route

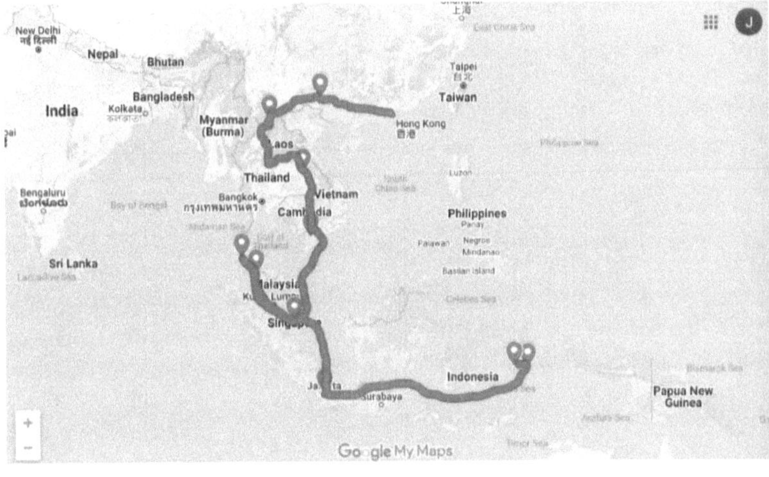

Chapter 1
Ray's Vow

They both heard the bump, almost a crunching sound. It sounded vaguely familiar, but they couldn't quite place it. At 2900 feet elevation, in the high desert air of the oil rich Permian Basin, sounds carried and could be misleading. It could have been down the block by the clock tower, or closer-in by the turning lane leading to the Odessa Police Station.

Sergeant George Wright had desk duty on this warm July morning, and Patrolman Bill Clark was at the corner desk, writing up the finishing touches of his report about last night's excitement. Curious, Bill walked over and opened the window, leaning out and looking down the street. The clock tower on the corner read 10:15 a.m. and 92 degrees Fahrenheit. There was an old yellow dog sleeping in the shade of the tower. The air was still, and the soft thump of oil pumpers could be heard. Bill sniffed the multiple odors of juniper, sage and crude oil. To him, it smelled good, like money. But what had made the noise?

Bill looked closer to the station, and muttered, "Ah, Jesus!"

George was suddenly alert. It was unusual for Bill Clark to curse, especially using the Lord's name in vain. Bill was a hardrock Southern Baptist, and very proper. George leapt to his feet and headed toward the window, alarmed. He said, "What?"

Bill looked at George with a bleak look, and said, "Miss Teel."

George spun on his feet to head toward the back door, muttering a more earthly profanity. "Shit."

Bill yelled at him, "George, goddamn it, don't run out on me! Look, she hit the same parking meter as last time. The city just got it fixed!"

As Miss Teel walked through the door, Bill was thinking he was going to hell for sure, all this cursing. But at least it stopped George from leaving.

Miss Teel stood in front of the two big policemen, all four-foot ten inches of her, with posture ramrod straight, every white hair in place, makeup perfect — just like they remembered her from years ago in her English class. The two men stood more or less at attention. This was not new to them, dealing with Miss Teel. They recalled struggling with the complexities of the English language in her eighth-grade class. Learning the parts of speech, conjugating verbs, diagramming sentences, writing essays, giving book reports — "For your own good," Miss Teel had assured them.

Miss Teel appraised them warmly, with a small smile. "Good morning, George, William. You boys always look good in your policeman's suits, but you've both gained a little weight since the last time I was in here."

Looking abashed, she said, "Oh, I hit the meter again. Maybe they should move them further in. I'll pay, just like last time." Then, glancing toward the door leading to the cells, she briskly continued, "Now, I've made Raymond's bail, and would like to visit with him, if I may."

They both ushered Miss Teel back toward the holding cells. On the way, she inquired about their families. She knew them all, as she had taught in Odessa for many years before she retired. At the cell door, after they opened it to let her in, she dismissed them with a stern glance. They left reluctantly, not wanting to miss the show.

"Maybe we can listen in," George murmured as they walked back down the hall.

Raymond James Murphy heard Miss Teel coming. He'd been expecting her, and struggled to get out of his bunk and make himself presentable. He looked pretty rough. Broken nose, two black eyes, and still bleeding from cuts in his mouth. He wasn't sure what to do about the blood, leaking out and occasionally dripping down his face. He didn't want to spit in front of Miss Teel. It didn't seem proper.

Miss Teel wasn't prepared for the sight of Ray. She gasped, stepped forward, and peered into his bloodshot eyes.

"Oh, Raymond. What happened to you?" she asked softly.

Raymond smiled through his bloody teeth and said, "We were discussing Alice Parker. RD told me to shut up, and I thought he said, 'Stand up.'"

She shook her head, "Goodness, Raymond. Are you talking about Rolando D. Carrera, in that hell-hole cantina of his, down in Little Mexico? You two are friends! You should quit fighting over Alice; both of you know better. She will cast both of you aside; she is looking for an easy life." Miss Teel frowned, "And are you gambling down there again?"

Ray looked at the floor and nodded, trying to look contrite. He liked the way her back arched when she was upset.

She stepped in closer, and got as eye-to-eye as her small frame would allow. "Raymond, you must change your ways. Your lifestyle in the oilfield is going to kill you. Gambling, drinking and fighting is all you seem to do anymore. You were one of the best students I ever taught. You have the skill to become a great writer."

She stepped still closer to him and raised her right hand to make a point. He'd seen the gesture many times before.

"Do you remember when you were playing summer league baseball? When you were at the top of your game, playing great, and the scouts came to town to see you? It was your chance to make it to the 'Bigs,' to have a major league career. But you didn't even make it to the game, you were in jail. And here you are again." Miss Teel shook her head and sighed. "How many oil companies in the Permian Basin will hire you anymore? And why, Raymond, why are you driving a taxi part-time in Little Mexico, taking drunks home at 2:00 a.m.?"

By this time, she was very close to him, leaning near as Ray sank back onto the bunk. Ray was shaken by her concern and intensity. Her perfume, he remembered, was called Rose Hip — though he could barely smell it. He saw tears in her eyes, and it caused him to try to breathe through his broken nose. He blew a blood bubble that splattered fine drops of blood on her face. Ray was horrified.

Her blood-specked face and tears warmed his heart, and he said through broken and bloody teeth, "I'm sorry, Miss Teel, I'll try to do better."

"You have such potential, Raymond. What you need to do, dear, is find something you are passionate about, then develop a dream, and follow that dream!"

Ray looked at her, as she wiped a finger across her cheek, leaving a trail of his blood. With the blood and her tears, his heart lurched.

He asked, "What's your passion, Miss Teel?"

She answered without hesitation. "Why, you are, Raymond, along with all my other students. You're still my students, even though I work at the library now. I want the best for you, and for you to do your best."

Ray nodded, with tears in his eyes. He vowed to himself that he would change his ways.

Miss Teel left as Ray was being processed out of jail. On the sidewalk, he breathed the air of freedom, and remembered his car was parked behind RD's cantina. He figured the twelve-block walk in the heat would help sweat out the booze, but his head hurt. Maybe a drink at RD's would help. Hair of the dog.

ROLANDO D. CARRERA was behind his bar when Ray walked in. It was early, and the cantina was empty, just the two of them.

RD was big, with thick black hair combed back, showing a widow's peak. He wore heavy black horn-rimmed glasses, and had unnaturally bleached white teeth, from lack of minerals. His voice sounded like broken glass. But his most telling feature was the two-hundred stitches in his face, from a long-ago automobile wreck. With his looks and fiery temperament, most everybody was afraid of RD except Ray Murphy. They were friends.

RD looked at Ray and said, "You alright?" as he put Ray's drink on the bar. Ray liked Greyhounds — vodka and fresh grapefruit juice, the fanciest drink at Carrera's bar.

"I'm okay," Ray said, "Can hardly breathe through this broken nose and my head hurts. What happened to your glasses?"

RD's glasses were taped together at the bridge and drooped over his nose. "You broke them, you fuck," RD said with no anger. "You hit me while you were going down."

Ray tried to smile, "Yeah, I remember tagging you just after I took your punch." He shook his head. "It was a good fight, RD, but you know it's not getting us anywhere."

RD nodded as he straightened his glasses. "You're right. Neither one of us is going anywhere with that bitch Alice. She's just having fun with us. We should just relax and enjoy it, because she's made it clear; her plan is to go to SMU in Dallas, marry a doctor, and work on her tan at her private pool for the rest of her life."

Ray was nodding, "Yep, she's a lost cause. We should move on." Ray was now behind the bar, putting ice on his nose. "I had a heart-to-heart talk with our Miss Teel this morning, and she's right, I need a change. I'm going to get a regular job and get away from the oil patch." His voice sounded pinched.

As Ray left, RD apologized for not getting him out of jail, saying that he barely escaped out the back when the cops arrived. Ray answered, "I know why you've got to keep your head down, brother. Judge Springer has a bead on you — you know he doesn't like Mexicans."

TRUE TO HIS WORD, RAY quit gambling and drinking so much, quit driving a taxi, and took an early morning job as a short-order cook at Shaw's Truck Stop Diner on Highway 20 just outside Odessa. Miss Teel had taught the owner, Wesley Shaw, and urged him to give Ray a chance. He went through a training period with the old cook who was wanting to retire, and was enthusiastic about his new profession.

Ray had always enjoyed cooking. He'd attended many chili cook-offs and was very interested in the ingredients and spices. At the Truck Stop, he began experimenting with various spices, and soon developed a red sauce that was good on almost anything. The truckers often requested it, and soon Ray was making large batches and trying different variations. Shaw's main complaint about Ray was the money he spent on spices, experimenting with new dishes. Ray would move up and down his row of spices, sniffing the different fragrances like an old redbone hound and commenting about them to the customers at the counter. Soon Ray Murphy became affectionately known as "The Spice Hound."

WESLEY SHAW PARKED by Ray's clunker in the far corner of the lot, and strolled toward his diner, through the cars and pickups, counting them. Nine pickups and four cars, plus two oil-field mud trucks, sitting by the highway, their engines idling. Not bad.

Wes grinned as he mentally tallied estimated revenues coming in from the early morning eaters. He especially liked to see the pickups and mud trucks, his repeat customers.

His new cook was doing okay for a rookie. He was certainly motivated, never late to the job and would stay late with no complaints if he was needed. Wes had seen him practicing breaking eggs with his left hand, while working the grill with the right. But he'd had his doubts when Ray spent $100 on spices the first week on the job. Ray said he'd read all about spices and cooking at the library.

Personally, Wes avoided libraries and churches because they put all kinds of fool notions in your head. For example, now Ray also wanted to write novels, another idea picked up in the library, in a how-to book he carried around. *"Shit, he's got lots of energy,"* Wes thought, *"you have to give him that, with that half-smile he always has that makes you wonder what he's thinking."* Funny how something always seemed to be happening around Raymond James Murphy.

The last thought proved true when Wes walked into his diner to see two of his best customers upset with Ray. Ival and Marvin, drivers of the mud trucks, sat at the counter in front of huge breakfasts that they were consuming with zest, spitting fine flakes of eggs and hashbrowns as they ate while complaining to Ray.

The McLarty brothers were not bookends. Ival, in his mud-splattered overalls and dented aluminum helmet, was bald, big and round. He wore a blue denim workshirt with the sleeves hacked off. Marvin was smaller and dapper, with the same dented helmet, but a clean Texas A&M sweatshirt and Levis. Ival spoke in a clear soprano, Marvin in a beautiful bass. Together they were giving Ray a verbal one-two punch, as the six tourist diners looked on nervously, some edging toward the exits.

"Goddammit Ray, you didn't have to kill us," Ival spewed, waving his knife at Ray.

Marvin's bass kicked in, "Yeah, what did we do to deserve that? We were great!" Counting off on his fingers, he continued, "We derailed the train, burned their cabin down, and shot them when they came out of the door. What more do you want?"

Wes had to stop a group of tourists at the door, saying "Relax, folks, it's just a story. These guys are characters in a novel that Ray, our cook —" he looked at Ray pointedly, "— is trying to write. Please stay, have more coffee and pie on the house."

Ray, with his chef's hat on, apologized from the grill. He tried to explain, both to the tourists and the brothers, what was going on, pointing at Ival and Marvin with his spatula.

"It's all just a story, guys. I used my friends as models for two characters, and, you know, novels need to build to a climax, and ..."

"We know, we know. It says all this in your how-to book," Ival interrupted, with his arms crossed. His meal was finished.

"What's that got to do with us?" Marvin asked. "I liked being in your book, and you killed us!"

"Well," Ray said, "You **were** the bad guys."

Chapter 2
French Girl?

In the corner of the diner by the window seat, Wes and Wanda Fay, the diner's manager, were eating breakfast, drinking coffee and discussing a serious problem about Julie, the cook on the second shift. She was pregnant, very pregnant.

Wes was saying, "I don't even like to check on the second shift anymore. I keep expecting her to gasp and grab her stomach." He shook his head. "Shit, I'd probably pass out."

Wanda Fay laughed her motherly laugh. She understood Wes because she mothered everyone, even Wes, her boss.

Stomachs full, they sat back in contented silence and watched the staff at work as they drank their coffee. Ray moved about in front of the grill on the balls of his feet, nodding as Sara called in the orders, cracking eggs with his left hand and pushing hashbrowns and meat around the grill with his right hand, holding a long-handled spatula. He never looked up at the orders clipped on the wire, doing it all from memory from her calls.

"Two over easy, bacon, browns," she would say, or "Omelet, no cheese, onions, grits, round pigs well done," etc.

As orders came off the grill, Ray would turn and place the plate under the proper ticket without looking. He moved with the fluid grace of an athlete, never apparently in a hurry, but he was fast, with orders spilling off the grill, always in proper sequence. As he worked, Ray would sing quietly to himself, barely audible to others. Today he was singing "Take me back to Tulsa, I'm too young to marry."

"He's good," Wanda Fay marveled, as she watched Ray in action, "and those spices ..."

"I hear you," Wes said, "That red sauce he makes, I swear, you could put it on a brick and eat it."

Wes shifted in his seat, "We need to get another cook for the second shift. I gotta send Julie home soon. I can hardly stand the stress. I have nightmares about delivering a baby in the kitchen of the diner."

Wanda Fay nodded in agreement, as she watched Sara giving change at the register. "I may have found someone that might even add a little class to this joint."

Wes was not offended by the comment. "Oh yeah?" he asked, "Who do you got?" He laughed. "We could use some class around here."

Wanda Fay leaned forward while lifting her cup to Sara for a refill. "Would you believe, a French girl, early twenties, a Cordon Bleu MasterChef?" She grinned. "Right here in beautiful Odessa, Texas!"

"You gotta be kidding. Is she lost?" Wes said.

Wanda Fay shrugged. "She may be lost, or at least carrying some baggage. Apparently, she was kicked out of a long-haul truck, out on Highway 20, while it was still moving. Banged her up pretty bad, but after two weeks at the Clinic, she needs a job."

"Jesus," Wes said, "Wonder what she said to get kicked out of a moving truck? You know how women ..."

Wanda Fay interrupted Wes with a little heat," Dammit, Wes, don't start going off about women talking too much. That shit don't get it anymore!"

Wes quickly nodded, sheepishly. He knew when to shut up. Not only was Wanda Fay the manager of his diner, she was also his aunt. Goddamn small towns anyway.

Chapter 3
Ray's Passion: Spices

As was his habit now, Ray was staying over after his shift to talk to Julie, the second shift cook, trying to learn more about the trade — she was a great cook. Julie looked up from her preparations as she noticed Ray.

Standing by the grill, putting on her apron, she said, "Thanks for cleaning the grill when you finish, Ray. The other cook didn't bother, most of the time."

"No problem," Ray said with a smile. "Do you mind if I ask a few questions?"

Julie nodded. "If you make them easy," she smiled.

"How pregnant are you?" Ray asked.

Julie gave him a look as she turned sideways to show him her profile, "I'm very pregnant, you dummy, can't you see? A woman can't be partly pregnant."

Ray laughed and held up his hands in surrender. "I'm sorry, Julie, I said that wrong. When is the baby due?"

"Three weeks, maybe sooner. Hopefully sooner," she smiled. Ray was forgiven.

"Are you going to have time to train the new cook?" Ray asked, as he helped her move the eggs, bacon and other foodstuffs closer to the grill for the afternoon's work. "I'm pretty new to be training her, even though Wes said she's some kinda MasterChef. Hell, not long ago, I was driving a taxi."

"Not to worry Ray, I can handle it, and with her background, she should be a quick study. But I can't imagine a Cordon Bleu-trained MasterChef moving from the Anatole Hotel kitchens in Dallas, to a roadside diner in Odessa. She must be desperate for money."

Ray was curious, "Do you think she will know a lot about spices?"

Julie said, "She should, since she's from France. You know, ironically, countries that have lived through the hardest times in their history have developed the best recipes. They had to, to survive. Look at what the Mexicans have done with flour, corn, water, some peppers, garlic, onions and a little meat. East Indians made curries and sauces. And the French have been at it for hundreds of years, using spices brought in on the Silk Road on camels, across China and Mongolia, from the Spice Islands in southeast Asia."

As they worked together, Julie continued, "You know, Ray, food wasn't that tasty in olden times. There was no way to keep it fresh. Spices helped delay rotting, and the flavors helped people choke down their less-than-fresh food. Some, like cinnamon, became very valuable, too, worth the price of a horse, cow, or goat, depending on the spice. Spices were even used for money at times, and became a status symbol for the wealthy."

Ray was dumbfounded. Her knowledge about spices amazed him. "How do you know all that about spices?" he blurted.

Julie smiled at him. "Would you believe I went to chef's school, too, before my husband came out here to get in the 'oil bidness?' Only my school was in Fort Worth, down by the stockyards," she laughed.

Ray shook his head in despair. It seemed everybody knew more about his new profession, and spices, than he did. He felt ignorant and unprepared. It was enough to drive you to drink.

WHEN THE NEW COOK ARRIVED the next morning and was introduced around, Ray started having problems. He put eggshells in an omelet, lost track of the orders, and burned himself on the grill. Even with scratches on her face, the woman was drop-dead beautiful, with long red hair, flashing green eyes, and the fairest skin he'd ever seen, with a sprinkling of freckles. Her eyes seemed to glow with energy and curiosity, and she gave him this look, ...

... with those pouty lips, just begging to be kissed. Ray was struck dumb. He was smitten. He was toast.

Ray left the diner with the melancholies, bummed because a lowly know-nothing short-order cook didn't stand a chance with the classy women of this world. It occurred to him that maybe a few Greyhounds would cheer him up. RD made the best Greyhounds in Odessa; half a pink grapefruit, squeezed over ice, with vodka. They were delicious, and after a few of them, you started calling them "Dawgs." A few would surely cheer him up.

When Ray walked into the cantina, RD was behind the bar, alone, as it was early.

"Hey, wetback," Ray said as he sat on a barstool.

"Hey, pendejo," RD smiled, turned and made Ray a Greyhound. With his scars and bleached-out teeth, RD was scary looking in the light of day or in the dark. The light behind the overhead fan flickered on his thick glasses. The bar was spotless, with the musky smell of incense to mask the odor of bleach. At the sides of the back-bar, unpainted corrugated sheet metal clad the walls, with bullet holes spread along their length in an uneven pattern. "Montezuma's Revenge" was written above the bullet holes in drippy red paint, or it could have been blood. It was the name of RD's cantina, his tongue-in-cheek way of poking fun at the world.

Cactus plants stood in the corners of the cantina. This was no fern bar. The high clear notes of Herb Alpert's Tijuana Brass could be heard in the background. Soft clattering of cutlery being washed emanated from the galley, with the fragrant whiffs of Mexican food. Behind the bar, within easy reach, a Model 97 Winchester 12-gauge pump shotgun hung on the wall. Although it blended in perfectly with the wall art, it was oiled, loaded, and the hammer was back. RD called it his bar sweeper. Above the barback was an original photograph of Pancho Villa and his gang, standing with their big sombreros, pistols and rifles.

Ray nodded at the picture as he took a drink, "You were born too late, RD. You would've rode with Pancho."

RD smiled, "Yeah, and I'd have been dead, with the moves I make."

Ray nodded in agreement, "Yeah, you've almost been dead a few times already."

Then he said, "Make me another greyhound, buddy, and I'll tell you about my new co-worker who starts next week. I met her today. Her name is Giselle, spelled with a G but said like a J, Sabo. She's from 'Gay Paree,' and she's drop-dead gorgeous. Eat your heart out." He laughed.

RD turned from mixing the drink, "Not Paris, Texas?" he asked innocently.

"Nope. She's from the big one over yonder. Learned to cook at some high-rent school in that other Paris. She speaks French, English and German, I saw on her application. She's twenty-three, weighs in at about one-hundred ten pounds, all in the right places, and she has green eyes and red hair that coils down her healthy front." Ray took the drink from RD and sipped.

"And RD, she's a flirt; I know, I can tell. Even with my 'training' with our friend Alice Parker, there's a chance this French one might eat me alive. I can hardly wait, but to tell you the truth, I'm a little scared of her, like I may be in over my head. I got so distracted today I nearly burned myself. But just so you know, RD, I'm not fighting you over Alice anymore. You can have her. I'm going to be busy."

RD laughed as he poured a drink for himself. "You sound like you have it bad. Let me know if you need any advice, or help."

RAY COULDN'T BELIEVE his good fortune. It had been decided by diner management (Wes and Wanda Fay) that the new cook would train during part of both the morning and afternoon shifts. This would allow training during breakfasts as well as dinners. Morning work on the grill changed in the afternoon, from breakfast fare to soups, salads and combination dinners. Both Julie and Ray would work with Giselle for a week or two.

Ray could hardly wait to be side by side with Giselle, but he was nervous. What if he pronounced her name wrong? It was Giselle with a "J," right? What if he couldn't understand her? He had never met anyone from France, would she have different interests? Should he get a haircut? On and on his thoughts went, through the weekend.

Chapter 4
Enter Giselle, and the Dream

On Monday morning, Giselle Sabo walked across the parking lot for her first day of work. She was dressed like a chef, in whites and comfortable half boots. Her bright red hair was braided and tied up in a white scarf. She wore another large scarf, a green one, around her neck.

As she approached the diner, Giselle thought about the chain of events that brought her to Odessa. The old camp trailer that Wes had provided for her, parked across the road under a pecan tree, was worlds apart from the apartment where she'd grown up on the Left Bank in downtown Paris. She missed the restaurants, bars and boutiques she had frequented along the Seine, as a student working her way through Le Cordon Bleu to become a MasterChef. She missed the crepes you could order through the windows at the sidewalk cafes. She missed the pace, the social life, the all-night partying with artists, writers, chefs, soldiers and boatmen. She liked them all.

But for Papa, she would still be in Paris. Who would have thought Papa, a Lt. General commanding 25,000 troops, would have had so much trouble dealing with his daughters. She smiled, remembering the conversation.

"You set his car on fire?" he had asked. "How could you do that?"

"It was easy, Papa. Some petrol and a match."

By this time, he was getting very red, like he always did.

She explained further, "The bastard was commuting all the way from Bordeaux to Paris in his new sports car to abuse Stella. So, I ended his commute."

Lt. General Sabo, "Papa," shook his head. Giselle was efficient, he had to admit. Stella idolized her older sister and dumped the boyfriend. But Giselle had to leave France for a while, maybe to the U.S.

Giselle thought her exposure to people from all walks of life in Paris would prepare her to work anywhere in the world. She knew she was impetuous, and somewhat spoiled by the good life in Paris, but thought the well-paid Chef's position at a luxury hotel in Dallas, called the Anatole, would do her good.

But adjusting to the Texas culture was difficult. So many things were so different than Paris. Texans wanted their steaks burned, and they put ketchup on everything — even at the Anatole! They ate pizza for a main meal. There were button-downed Baptist-types on the one hand, and "Good-Ole-Boy" cliques on the other. The women had huge stiff hairdos and wore lots of blue eyeshadow and makeup. Texans talked mostly about the price of oil, the price of beef, football and politics. They drank Scotch whiskey and complained about wetbacks coming across the Rio Grande and taking jobs, and how "Texas negras" are better behaved than those up north — like they were pets. Regarding pets, Texans picked up dog shit off the sidewalks, crazy! You could get arrested here for peeing in the grass, something often seen in Paris. And they were inhibited about sex. They didn't understand the concept of sport fucking. And mon Dieu! If you suggest a menage-a-trois — you would go to jail for sure.

AS GISELLE ENTERED the diner, she was met by Ray Murphy, the cook that was to kick off her training during the breakfast shift. He gave her a nice smile. He had the look of an athlete, reminding her of a soccer player she'd once dated. He had dancing eyes and his broken nose and facial scars spoke of a life well spent.

She thought, *"Oh my, he might be fun."*

Ray had been preparing to meet Giselle all morning. First, he had checked with Wanda Fay to make sure he knew how to pronounce her name, with a "J." Next, he arranged the grill area so they could work together there. He made sure his spice rack was squared away, and watered the window box where he'd planted herbs, to Wes' amusement.

When Giselle walked in the door and Ray greeted her, he noticed her eye arch a little as she checked him out. She ran her tongue along her upper lip and smiled at him.

"Oh my," he thought, *"She might be fun."*

The training went well. Giselle was quick to learn the routine and had no trouble with the fast pace of short-order cooking. She tended to undercook the meat; a French thing, Ray guessed. Julie agreed, and they worked with Giselle to teach her to "burn it." They laughed a lot and Ray loved her accent. After only a week, Giselle was ready to take over Julie's shift.

In celebration, Ray took Giselle out to dinner at the Montezuma's Revenge cantina. RD was on hand, like a waiter, with a towel over his arm, checking Giselle out. Ray introduced him as his friend, not a waiter. RD brought complimentary margaritas to start.

Though they had worked together for a week, they hadn't had much time to get to know each other. Ray wondered about her truck accident and wounds. She still had abrasion marks on the side of her face, and walked with a slight limp.

"Have you pretty much recovered from your fall?" Ray asked.

Giselle smiled, "Yes, I'm much better now. I had a concussion and I'm over that, but still have headaches." She shrugged, "And my knee is getting better, but it has to be wrapped for a while longer."

She looked closely at Ray. "How about you? The scars on your face must tell a story or two."

Ray smiled. He was almost shy with this woman, with her sophistication, accent and worldly ways. He felt like a country hick. He vowed to answer her question as best he could.

He said, "You may not know much about baseball, America's national sport, but we wear cleats, you know, like on a soccer player's shoes?"

She nodded yes, with that teasing smile.

"In baseball," he continued, "You can steal bases, by running from bag to bag without getting tagged out by a thrown ball. I would slide in headfirst to touch the base before my opponent, and sometimes I'd hit the baseman's cleats." He pointed to the scars on his forehead. "Cleat marks."

"Ouch," she said, "Why headfirst?"

He realized she was very smart. "Quicker," he said with a smile.

She peered at him with a little squint. "Somehow, I think you always go in headfirst."

Ray nodded. He thought she wasn't talking just about baseball.

He continued, "Then, this scar," pointing to the half moon scar on his cheek, "A broken pool cue." He grinned, "From a celebration right here that turned into a brawl, and the chipped front tooth from that barstool over there." He pointed out the barstool.

Giselle tilted her head back and looked down her nose at him, with a knowing smile and nod. "No scars from work, only play. You like to play very hard, eh?"

Ray thought, *"Goddamn, this woman is something else."*

They were drinking margaritas, and had been for a while. It was 2-for-1 night, and four big glasses were on the table, mostly empty.

Ray had to ask, "How did it happen, Giselle?"

She was very direct. "Mike Holland, my lover, was showing me some of Texas on his delivery route. He and I had an argument, and he pushed me out of the truck at twenty miles an hour." She laughed, "Merde, I'm glad he slowed down."

She finished her drink, settled into the corner of the booth, looked at Ray and tried to explain.

"I have never felt the urge to 'mother' someone before, but big, healthy Mike Holland needs mothering. For some reason I felt compelled to help Mike deal with his fears. It's a side of me I didn't know existed. Up to now, I've been a self-serving party girl. But Mike brought something out in me, and I felt good about helping him. It made me better, you see?" She grabbed Ray's glass and took a healthy swallow, "That is why I left the hotel job for a road trip with Mike."

Ray was puzzled. He looked closely at Giselle and asked, "Mike Holland needed mothering?" as he thought, *"I could use some mothering from this little mama myself."*

Her answer surprised him. "Mike is a big strong man, but he carries many fears with him. I tried to help him with these fears," she said. "He fears the government will take away his freedoms and his right to bear arms, as he calls it."

She took another drink from Ray's glass and nibbled on her pecan praline, nodded and said, "mmm, good," and then continued, "Mike has all manner of guns with many boxes of ammunition stacked in his house and truck. He meets in the woods with his friends, and they practice with their guns and study military maneuvers because they think hordes of Mexicans, Negroes and Jews will overrun the country and take over. He said they fear gun control legislation will limit their rights guaranteed by the Second Amendment."

Giselle grinned at Ray and said, "To me, Mike and his friends are like scared little boys, always worrying and looking over their shoulders." Giselle shook her head. "When I told him this, and advised him not to be so afraid, he got upset with me and tossed me out of his truck." With a glint in her eye she said, "It's his loss. I loved him."

Looking at their empty glasses, Ray said, I really want to invite you to my apartment for a drink, but I'm afraid it's impossible."

Giselle looked at him curiously. "Why?"

Ray sheepishly grinned, "I found this neat apartment over a flower shop. It's inexpensive and I liked that it's on a hill."

Giselle looked skeptically at the west Texas landscape, and asked "You liked the hill for the view?"

Ray laughed. "What view? No, my car doesn't always start, so with a hill I can push it off, pop the clutch, and get it going. As you can see, it's an old forty horsepower VW Beetle, so it's easy to push off."

Giselle frowned and asked, "So, ... it's impossible to visit your apartment because your car might not start?"

"No, not that," Ray said, "It's the roaches."

Giselle's eyes widened and her lip came up, "Roaches?"

"Yep," Ray nodded, "The reason the nice apartment was so cheap is because armies of roaches invade from the flower shop below. They slither across the floor, day and night. I can hear them in the walls. Sometimes I find them in my bed. I've put out poison, but it hasn't worked yet."

Giselle was shaking her head, and her lip was still up. She looked down at the table, wet from the moisture of many margarita drinks. As Ray was talking, he'd drawn an arrow through the puddle, pointing directly at her left breast. She wondered if he'd drawn the arrow subconsciously. She looked at his dancing eyes. No, he'd drawn it on purpose. This boy was hungry.

"Better idea, Ray, why don't we go to my trailer for a drink? But it's not on a hill."

SO, THE ROMANCE BEGAN. Giselle and Ray made love far into the night. To Giselle, it was sport fucking with an interesting guy. To Ray, doors were being opened to a level of passion beyond his comprehension. He was consumed by the experience and felt like following Giselle around like a puppy.

Later, laying in a tangle of bedding, Giselle smiled saucily and said, "I was right about you, Ray. You go in headfirst."

Ray blushed for the first time in his life.

"Would you like to sit out by the pecan tree and listen to music? It's cooler out there with the breeze."

They ate chips, drank Lone Star beer out of an ice chest, and looked for music on the portable radio. There was no music, just some dude recapping the first six months of 1990 — Nelson Mandela released from prison, the Berlin Wall coming down, and the Hubble Space Telescope sending the first pictures from outer space.

"Some year so far, huh?" Ray said. "I think it may be the best year of my life."

Giselle leaned back in the lawn chair and said, "Are the roaches really that bad at your place?"

Ray's chin went up and down, "Yep. It's worst when you first turn the lights on — they're all over the floor, scrambling to get out of the light. Creepy."

"So it wasn't a lie, to get into my camper?"

"Giselle, know this," Ray said, "I'm a straight shooter, coming right at you, no lies, no way."

Giselle smiled, "Hanging with you will be a new experience, then."

RAY AND GISELLE EXTENDED their hours at the diner so their shifts would overlap, giving them time to visit as they worked. Giselle taught Ray different cooking tricks and techniques.

Giselle told Ray, "Food is life, and spices and herbs make life spicy and fun. I believe every ingredient affects your health and well-being. Herbs and spices have been used for centuries, not just for taste, but as medicines. We are responsible for improving the lives of everyone who eats our food." Ray was transfixed.

The nights were theirs, and they made the most of it. They drank, they partied, and they pursued their common interest in spices. Giselle had her favorites, including saffron and Herbes de Provence. She loved saffron for its flavor and color, but also because it was the most expensive spice in the world. "Herbes de Provence" was new to Ray, so she explained the combination of herbs, many of them growing in Ray's window boxes.

They became interested in the origin of spices — especially the Spice Islands, such as Malaku, Ambon and Banda. These islands were in southeast Asia, in the Indonesian island chain. From a book that Ray borrowed from the library, they learned that the Spice Islands were where the major spice trade had all started, from forests abundant with nutmeg, mace, cloves and pepper. They learned about cinnamon, peeled from the inner bark of a tree, and the ugly ginger root with it's beautiful flowers. These exotic plants, discovered in the islands by the Portuguese in 1512, followed closely by the profit-hungry Dutch, precipitated the camel trains on the Silk Road to the Mediterranean ships, bound for European markets.

Ray and Giselle researched the Spice Islands, put maps of them on the wall, and dreamed of visiting them someday. In an emotional moment, they vowed that, if ever separated, they would meet in the Spice Islands. To Ray, this was all exotic high adventure on a grand scale, a long way from Odessa, Texas. He took the vow to heart. Of course, Ray was influenced by Giselle, the ultimate spice.

IT WAS EARLY AFTERNOON and the cantina was quiet. Ray and RD were in a booth, discussing high finance. Not long after Ray's last jail visit, he discovered a red shop rag in the front seat of his VW, tied at the corners. In it was writing on a bar coaster, and a roll of bills in the amount of $500. On the coaster was written, "Help you out."

"RD, let me pay you back, I can pay $100 a month, easy."

"The money wasn't a loan," RD said, "Remember, I was the other half in that dustup. If you hadn't slowed them down by bleeding all over that deputy, I would have got caught, and Judge Springer would have shut me down!"

"But $500 ..." Ray started.

"Cheap at twice the price," RD said, "We had fun, didn't we?"

"Fun. I don't remember that part. And why are you grinning at me like that, ever since I came in, you crazy Mexican?"

RD grinned even more, "Let me get you another Dawg, Ray, and maybe you can tell me why you've been seen re-blocking Wes' camp trailer, twice!"

Ray blushed for the second time in his life, and RD cracked up, sounding like a donkey braying. It had been the talk of the bar.

Ray looked at his drink, "My God, RD, some of the things we've been doing in that camper, I'm sure, would get us arrested in the Great State of Texas. But even if they shot me for it, I'd die smiling.

He shook his head in wonderment, with a sheepish grin. RD laughed again.

Ray went on, "She's quite a woman. It's more than just great sex; she's smart, a great cook, and interesting, and fun, and ...."

"Oh man, Ray. I think you've really got it bad!"

RAY AND GISELLE RESEARCHED the Spice Islands in more depth at the library. Miss Teel helped them, finding history and travel books, cookbooks and maps. Miss Teel was proud of Ray's lifestyle changes, and credited Giselle with "settling him down." She thought they made a cute couple, but she could feel the heat coming off them. It brought back memories ...

As they studied the spices, Giselle and Ray collected more topographical maps of the Spice Islands, and learned about the people who lived there, their culture, geography, vegetation, latitude and longitude, tides and currents, prevailing winds, temperatures, best approaches by boat, etc. Tropical and remote, the islands sounded like a perfect spot to visit. As they collected the data, they became more motivated to see the islands and walk among the spices that grew there — like no other place in the world. They tried to learn more about the Dutch caretakers of the islands, but the information was limited.

"Ray, I would love to visit the islands to see how the people live." Giselle said, "There must be wonderful health benefits from living among the source of these spices — I've heard that ancient cultural medicines used herbs and spices to cure ills and promote good health. And can you imagine the smells? Cinnamon, nutmeg, vanilla!"

"Too bad the Dutch don't seem to like tourists," Ray said.

Ray and Giselle continued to experiment with various spices in their cooking and built up an extensive spice rack. Giselle also got into herbal teas, and tried different blends.

"Tea is one of the best ways to get the goodness of plants and herbs," she would say. "Try this tea."

And she would hand him her latest mixture. Some blends were very good and went on the shelf, others were foul-tasting and were tossed out after they dared each other to take another sip.

With Wes, Ray began a sideline business of bottled hot sauces, sold at the diner. RD had Ray make Mexican-style appetizers to serve at Montezuma's Revenge. Giselle added to the diner's afternoon menu, and they started occasional full sit-down dinners. Miss Teel was thrilled, and became a frequent taste-tester for the couple. They built up their own library of recipes from books oriented to the spices they preferred. They experimented with dish after dish, and tried them out on people. Business at the diner grew as the patrons raved about the exotic meals Giselle and Ray served.

Chapter 5
Heartbreak

Sundown in Odessa, and Ray headed for Giselle's. He'd showered and togged up for an evening of socializing. As he worked through the gears of his old VW, he thought of last night's adventure with a smile. It was too hot inside the trailer so they'd moved outside, and damn near killed themselves in the hammock. As they hit the ground, they noticed a coyote lying in the brush watching the show. They'd tried to run him off, but he would hardly leave — making it all the funnier. They'd laughed hysterically. As Ray reminisced and approached the trailer, he didn't notice the big semi with a sleeper cab parked by the road.

Giselle was sitting on the front steps waiting for him, two full pillowcases beside her. Ray slowly walked towards her, feeling uneasy. She looked different.

Giselle spoke first, "Mikey is back."

Ray tilted his head, "Who? Mikey?"

"Oui, he has come back for me. I'm going with him."

Ray couldn't believe what he was hearing. "Mike Holland, the same guy that pushed you out of his truck?"

"Oui," she said again, through clenched teeth.

"Giselle, how can you go with this guy after all we have done together? After what he did to you?" Ray almost choked. "I don't understand."

Giselle stood up, holding the pillowcases full of clothes, and said, "Mikey needs me, and I love him." She smiled a little wistfully. "And I can leave you after all the good times we had — because I'm French!"

She set down the pillowcases to give him a long erotic kiss, then picked them up, walked over to the truck and climbed into the cab. She didn't look back. The truck left immediately, going through the gears, headed west.

Ray sat on the porch for two hours, listening to the thump of the pumpers, looking at the last of the sunset, and thinking about what happened. Then he grabbed a sixpack of Lone Stars from the camper's fridge and headed home to get ready for his early morning shift. He felt like his heart was broken.

RAY WAS AT HIS GRILL at 6:00 a.m. the next morning, taking care of the early breakfast crowd. He wasn't singing. Even the customers seemed subdued. When Wes came in at 10:00 to make his rounds, Ray motioned him over.

"Giselle's gone," he said, looking Wes in the eye.

Wes was stunned. "What? Just like that?" he asked.

"Yep. She left with the same trucker that tossed her out of his rig. He came back and said he needed her."

Ray could tell Wes was already thinking about a cook for the second shift.

"Wes, I'll work Giselle's shift too, hold it open for her, for when she comes back. After working in the oilfield, the long hours won't hurt me. I don't have anything else I want to do now, anyway."

THE MARATHON HOURS didn't seem to faze Ray, even as the days passed. He cooked like he was on autopilot, thinking of other things. There were no longer specials, no dinner events, no new recipes. He was very quiet. Wes encouraged him to take some time off, but Ray refused.

No word was heard from Giselle Sabo; it was like she never existed. RD Carrera began stopping by the diner fairly regularly. He never said much, and only nodded to Ray occasionally. Everyone knew RD was worried and was checking up on Ray. Miss Teel even stopped by several times "for tea." The truckers Marvin and Ival couldn't even get a rise out of Ray as they heckled him to put them in more of his novels.

After Ray had worked double shifts for two weeks, Wes was getting concerned.

"Ray," he said, "How much longer can you keep this up? Sixteen hour days can wear you down, and also, my letting you work this much might be illegal, you know? I don't think she's coming back, you need to move forward."

Ray gave a small smile, "The work's not hurting me, Wes. You wouldn't believe the hours we worked in the oilfields. Also," he added, "Giselle could walk through that door anytime now. Surely, she's not going to hang with that needy trucker forever."

As he finished cleaning the counter, Ray asked, "Where did you send her last check? She had two weeks coming, right?"

"Yup. I just got a forwarding address in Paris from the Anatole Hotel. I'll be forwarding the check to that address soon."

"Could I include a letter to her with the check?" Ray asked, and Wes nodded.

RAY SPENT HOURS CRAFTING a letter to Giselle, telling her the job was here for her when she returned. He promised they would take a tramp freighter to southeast Asia, to see the Spice Islands, like they had dreamed. He told her he loved her and would be here for her when she returned. The next day, his letter was included with the check being mailed to Giselle's forwarding address in Paris.

Ray felt much better. Now all he had to do was wait for Giselle to return.

Chapter 6
Loss, and a Quest

Five weeks after Giselle's departure, Ray was working the grill when Julie came in.

She stood, watching him work for a while, then said, "Ray, I want my old job back. You're killing yourself doing double shifts and I need the work to put my new baby girl through school. I am, by God, going to send her to Texas A&M to become a veterinarian."

Ray smiled, "Look at you, Julie, you're on fire to pave the way for your little daughter. I admire you for that. So, I will officially turn the spatula over to you. The world needs more veterinarians. When Giselle comes back, she can have my shift, and I'll go back to the taxi."

"Giselle ain't coming back, Ray."

"Oh yeah, she's coming back. She just needs time to sort things out," Ray said.

Patting his back, Julie said with a sad smile, "Ray, you look very tired. Enjoy your afternoons off. Go see RD."

TWO WEEKS LATER, ON a Friday, Odessa was in the midst of a bodacious windstorm. Tumbleweeds were streaking across the highway at twenty miles an hour, stacking up on fences and bowling them over. Blowing sand was everywhere, in your mouth, eyes and ears, gumming up machinery, creeping under windows and doors, and all over the furniture. The air smelled of crude oil, juniper, sage, fresh dirt and cow shit.

It was mid-morning, and Ray was cooking an omelet, thinking about the proper spice for it. He favored his red chili sauce, but it might be too much for the Yankee-looking tourist, looking at him from the booth.

Suddenly, Ray noticed the diner had become quiet. He looked up to see Miss Teel walking through the door, looking at him. Even the wind and dust hadn't fazed her. Every hair was in place. But she looked somber.

"Ray, please step outside with me."

"What? In this wind, Miss Teel?"

"Let's go through the kitchen, out back," she said.

Ray motioned to Henry, the trainee cook and dishwasher, to finish the omelet, and led Miss Teel out back. There was a bench in the lee of the wind by a dumpster. Ray was worried.

"Miss Teel, are you okay?"

She motioned Ray to sit on the bench next to her, and leaned over to put her arm across his shoulders. Now Ray was really worried, as this was most unusual for Miss Teel.

She looked at him intently. "You know, at the library we get newspapers from all over. This morning, I was reading the Denver Post ..."

Miss Teel sighed, looked down and took his hand. "Ray, there was a wreck two weeks ago. A long-haul truck hit black ice, jackknifed, rolled and burned. No survivors. Giselle was identified from personal effects. Giselle has been killed, Ray. I'm so sorry."

Ray sat hunched over on the bench as if he'd been punched in the stomach. He looked at the dumpster. Miss Teel waited.

"I just knew she would be back," he said. Tears trickled down his cheeks. He looked up at Miss Teel and said, "I better go check on that omelet," but he didn't move.

He took a deep breath and wiped his eyes. "Where did it happen?"

"The paper said Idaho Springs, thirty miles west of Denver."

Ray stood up, hugged Miss Teel, then turned and went back to the grill.

EARLY THE NEXT MORNING, Ival and Marvin walked into the diner for their usual monster breakfasts. Their mud trucks were parked by the road, catching tumbleweeds. The wind was still blowing hard, wearing everybody out.

"Fucking wind!" Ival said, as he crawled onto the bar stool, looking for Ray to harass. "My diesel bill doubles, driving into that wind."

Marvin sat beside him, looking at the menu. Ival noticed Wanda Fay was working the grill.

"Where's Ray?" he asked.

Wanda Fay looked at the brothers over the grill. She'd known them all her life.

"Ray went to Colorado to bury Giselle. I told him it's been over three weeks and she's probably already in the ground, but he went anyway. He caught a semi headed west, picked him up in about fifteen minutes. Not surprising, since he sits in the booths with the truckers on his breaks. Knows them all."

Marvin and Ival were shocked, and both looked at Wanda Fay.

"Giselle? What happened? How'd she die?" they asked in unison.

Wanda Fay pointed at the mud trucks, "Black ice, a jackknife, roll and burn."

The brothers grimaced.

"Black ice! Goddamn that high Yankee country, anyway. Man, she was a pretty woman. What a shame," Marvin said.

TWO DAYS LATER, RAY was hiking to the City Cemetery in Idaho Springs, Colorado, looking for a new grave. He'd made the trip from Odessa in two rides, and had slept as he rode in the trucks. He wasn't tired. The grave was easy to spot, with fresh dirt heaped up, by a cottonwood tree and a bench. Ray figured a headstone was on its way later. Or maybe not.

Ray walked up to the grave, unsheathed his equipment, and started urinating on the grave, below a temporary plaque that read "Michael Holland." It was a long, satisfying piss; he'd saved it up from the last coffee shop.

"Motherfucker, you killed my woman," he muttered aloud as he finished and shook himself off.

Ray heard a chuckle, and turned to see RD Carrera sitting on the bench. RD wore a black leather jacket with many zippers, jeans, and highly polished boots with metal tipped toes.

RD said, "I gotta say, Ray, you are a class act."

"What are you doing here?" Ray blurted. "How did you find me?"

RD teed off, "Well, even though you didn't tell **anybody anything**, your **friends** pieced it together. The rest was easy. I got a CB radio in my ride, and talked to the truckers, high technology. This is the 90's, dude."

He pointed to his Lincoln Mark VII with the whip antenna, at the gate, its twin exhaust pipes showing white. RD always drove flat out, and collected tickets like socks.

"Ray, I'm really sorry about Giselle. She was a neat lady."

Ray looked sadly at RD. "She's not even here anymore. I just missed her. A couple of days ago, her remains were picked up at the Denver airport by a Lear 36 corporate jet with French markings, and flown to Paris."

RD was impressed. "Wow. Who arranged that?"

"The guy at the funeral home was very understanding and spent some time with me. Once they identified Giselle, the cops contacted her family. Bert, at the funeral home, said a French Lieutenant General Sabo organized everything."

RD whistled. "Wow. Three stars, the dude is a heavy hitter for sure. Three-star Generals are like gods."

"Do you think he would blame me for Giselle's death?" Ray asked.

As they got into the Mark VII, RD said, "Ray, you didn't kill Giselle, you weren't even in the same state. You just pissed on the guy who was responsible. But, if a three-star General wants you, even if he's French, you are probably toast."

Ray shook his head. "Man, that's comforting."

On the ride home Ray was quiet, still grieving and trying to get his head around all that had happened. RD was entertaining himself by outrunning the Colorado Highway Patrol. A cop picked them up at a speed trap while they were only going twenty miles over the speed limit. With red and blue lights flashing behind them, RD took off. He buried the needle with the Lincoln doing about 130, trying to reach the Oklahoma panhandle ahead of the cops. The panhandle was a refuge. No cop in their right mind would patrol the Oklahoma panhandle.

They were running the back roads now, as the cops got more excited, and more numerous. They topped a hill at speed and the Lincoln became airborne, landing a little sideways. The tires chirped and the car brushed a guardrail in the turn. RD glanced at Ray and saw he was completely relaxed. RD grinned, showing his stained teeth.

"You show no fear, brother."

"You're a pure soul, RD, and the gods protect you. The Devil has already taken a few shots at you and missed. I figure that after all I've been through, I may now be protected too, so I'm comfortable going along for the ride."

"Have you come to terms with Giselle's death?" RD asked, as he steered the car around another turn.

Ray looked at the telephone poles whipping by, and tried to estimate their speed.

"No, RD, I'm frustrated. I hardly got to say 'bye' to her when she took off, now she's dead and I can't even pay my respects. There's no evidence that she even existed. I was given a chance to love her, and now she's been snatched away, gone forever, in the blink of an eye." He shook his head. "What can I do in her memory? I ask myself."

"Ray, you've come a long way since you met Giselle. I miss our crazy times."

The serious conversation ended abruptly as they crossed the Oklahoma border, whooped in celebration, and headed home.

BACK IN ODESSA, RAY went to Giselle's camp trailer to clean it out for Wes. When he walked in the door, the smell of Giselle's perfume caused him to choke up. He looked through her things and it got worse for him. She'd departed in a hurry and left little things here and there that triggered memories. He looked at the maps of the Spice Islands they'd pinned on the wall, and the piles of notes and recipes. He started drinking the last of the Lone Star beers as he moved around the camper.

The weather had moderated, so he moved outside to the hammock to finish off the beers. As he lay in the hammock, the coyote slowly moved into his regular place to watch him. Remembering it all, Ray cried as he and the coyote looked at each other in the twilight.

Ray slept for two hours in the hammock, then went into the camper to look at the Spice Island maps again. He studied them for a long time, then leaned forward and tapped his head on the maps. In that moment, he made his decision.

Ray rented the trailer from Wes, to stay in until a new cook was found. He sold or gave away all his belongings except what would go in one suitcase. He visited his family and gave his VW to his little brother. He was getting ready to go to the Spice Islands, in a shared memory with Giselle Sabo. Raymond James Murphy was going on a quest.

Chapter 7
Starting the Quest

Ray was hitchhiking, sitting on his suitcase by the Mr. Peanut sign on Highway 20. The bug-looking guy, supposed to be a peanut, with a top hat, monocle and cane, the Planter's Peanut logo, was looking down on him in the moonlight. It was 1:00 a.m., cool and quiet, and traffic moving east past Odessa was infrequent.

He was dozing off when a big Chrysler 300 came flying across the shoulder of the road, just missing him, sliding sideways through the sign, knocking boards into the air with a huge crash. The boards and bits came raining back down, landing on Ray and the car, which had reversed itself, shearing off the signposts. The car ended up with its headlights still on, facing out the way it had come.

Ray made his way through the trail of debris to the driver, who was sitting looking out the windshield like he was at a drive-in movie, his eyes large. He wasn't moving.

"You alright?" Ray asked, then added, "The first thing I saw when I woke up, was Mr. Peanut on those boards, coming down on me."

The driver, a small balding man with a short beard, shook himself and said, "That's the first thing I saw when I woke up, too."

They looked at each other, like, maybe this will be funny later.

"You hitchhiking?" the man asked, giving Ray an appraising look. When Ray nodded, the driver continued, "Would you be willing to trade off driving to Dallas? I've driven straight through from San Diego, and I'm worn out. I'm in a hurry."

Ray looked at him evenly, "You runnin' from the law?"

"No, not at all," he shook his head, then held it in both hands. "My name is Abe Klein, and I'm a diamond trader." He dropped his hands and looked at Ray steadily. "My brother recently died in Dallas in the middle of a diamond transaction, and I need to get there as quick as I can. Can you help me?"

Ray looked at the car. There was no visible damage other than dents and scratches on the hood and side door. No gas or oil on the ground, and only one diagonal crack across the windshield. Abe looked okay too, except for a bloody nose. Abe struggled to pull out his handkerchief and dab at it.

"That hurts, don't it? You may have black eyes tomorrow, too." Ray said. "Hey, I'll help you if we don't speed. I don't aim to get killed on the way to Dallas in a Chrysler, when I really want to go to Houston, anyway. It's hard to go direct to Houston from Odessa. I'd hoped to cut across on 87 at Big Spring."

Sopping at his large nose, Abe said, "You help me get to Dallas, I'll pay your way to Houston."

Ray gave a little smile. "Bus or plane?"

AS THEY STRUGGLED TO get the car out of the debris, Abe realized he didn't know if the kid could even drive. He looked about twenty, but had a capable, direct way about him. The way he carried himself, Abe figured he was descended from the goddamn scrappy Irish.

"What's your name?" he asked.

When Ray said, "Ray. Raymond Murphy," Abe thought, *"Irish. I knew it."*

They got the Chrysler on the road. Ray got behind the wheel and Abe settled in the passenger seat. The steering pulled left, and the right door made a sucking sound if they went past 70, which would keep them from going too fast. Abe was weary and wanted to sleep, but felt the need to talk a bit, to take the kid's measure and make sure he was an okay driver.

"What do you do, Ray?"

Ray shrugged. "I'm a short-order cook, amongst other things. I'd like to get a job on a freighter in Houston, headed for southeast Asia." He adjusted the seat and mirrors of the Chrysler, like he knew what he was doing.

"And you're a diamond trader? How does that work?" Ray asked. He seemed curious.

"Yes, we buy raw uncut diamonds from South Africa, Namibia and, would you believe, Canada, and cut them to add value for trading." He could see Ray nodding, interested.

Ray smoothly accelerated to 65 and held it there, like it was pegged. He eased the Chrysler around a loaded semi, gave it plenty of room and flicked his lights in thanks to the trucker. He was a good driver. They passed a road sign that said 364 miles to Dallas. Abe leaned back in the seat and fell into an exhausted sleep. He dreamed about his brother in happier times.

Two hours later, with Abe awake, the conversation started again. Fueled by fatigue and grief on Abe's part, and by grief, the excitement of freedom, and fear of the unknown on Ray's part, more was said than under normal circumstances. The mood was also enhanced by the road's late-night sights, sounds and smells — the bolting jackrabbits and coyotes, the slap of tires on pavement, and the smell of juniper, sage and melted tar patches from the heat.

Ray asked the first question with such curiosity in his voice, that Abe was surprised. "Abe, what happened to your brother?"

Abe shook his head, "If what I'm told is true, the circumstances of his death are unbelievable and extremely sad. I can hardly think about it without breaking down."

"If you don't want to talk about it, that's okay. I was just curious."

"Maybe if I talk about it, it will help," Abe said. "My brother and I source and trade diamonds, but we are also cutters. If a rough diamond can be cut properly, its value is enhanced enormously. We like to trade finished diamonds for rough cuts, and do our own magic."

Abe held a handkerchief to his nose. It had quit bleeding, and he could breathe better. "Of course, to trade diamonds, we have to transport them, which can be expensive and risky. Many times, we move them ourselves in our cars. Very risky. Your whole financial future can be tied up in the trunk of your car. But if you can pull it off, you can save a lot of money. Guarded transport and professional security are very expensive."

"So, you guys are bootlegging the diamonds to save money?" Ray asked.

Abe cringed at this description, but said, "In essence, yes."

"And your brother got hijacked?"

"No. The diamonds are fine. That's the horrible part of the story. Let me explain." Abe sighed. "My brother likes the Anatole Hotel in Dallas."

"My girlfriend used to work there," Ray said, picturing Giselle preparing meals for Abe's brother. He shook his head quickly, to stop the thoughts. "But please, tell me what happened."

Abe resumed his story, "Daniel liked the good security and well-lit parking lots at that hotel. He parked the car under the lights, with diamonds locked in the trunk, and went to his room on the fifteenth floor. He slept well, called me and talked about the meeting scheduled with the other trader." Abe paused and almost choked.

Ray looked at him apprehensively. "What happened?"

Abe answered in a different voice, almost pleading and drawn out, "My brother has always been excitable and impulsive. That morning, Daniel went out on the balcony, which at the Anatole sort of twists around an abutment. He wanted to check on the car in the parking lot — and it wasn't there. The car was gone," Abe continued, almost in a whisper now.

"When he saw the empty parking lot, and realized everything was lost, Daniel, my brother," Abe choked, ".... jumped off the balcony of the fifteenth floor."

The car was slowing down, and Ray was looking at Abe, his face flushed. "What? The car was stolen?"

"No," Abe said, his eyes tearing. "That's the worst part. The car was fine, it was where it was supposed to be. My brother was looking at the wrong parking lot."

Abe looked up to see the car nosing into a truck stop cafe.

Ray said, "That's horrible. We need a break. Let's get some pie and coffee, or maybe a drink."

RAY AND ABE SETTLED into a booth at the truck stop, with huge pieces of apple pie and coffee mugs with 'US Navy' stenciled on them, almost worn off from years of use. The jukebox was blaring a Charley Pride song, and they could hear a spirited argument from the kitchen. Huge over-the-road trucks were maneuvering back and forth by the diesel pumps. An enormous bomber's moon glowed over the sagebrush. Sleepy-eyed truckers slouched in the other booths, mostly alone, looking past their food with thousand-yard stares.

Abe poured two overly full spoons of sugar in his coffee, gave a sad smile and said, "You've heard my story, Ray. How about you? What's your story? You look like you've lived a bit, for a pretty young guy."

"I've been in Odessa all my life, worked in the oilfields, drove a taxi and recently was a short-order cook at the diner not far from where you drove your Chrysler through the Mr. Peanut sign. The scars are from playing ball and partying too hard while I was young."

Abe nodded. "So, I'm curious. Why do you want to get a job on a freighter to southeast Asia? It's a long way from Texas."

Ray gave a sad little smile, and said, "This amazing French girl and I worked together at the diner, she's the one who used to work at the Anatole. We loved spices and cooking with them, and we became interested in visiting the Spice Islands. So, I aim to go there."

"What about her? She's not going?" Abe asked.

When Ray answered, Abe saw his lips tremble, "Um, no. She's with her father in Paris."

"You're going alone? She's not joining you in the Spice Islands?"

Ray paused for a long moment, then looked out at the big moon, sighed deeply, then slowly started with a bigger and bigger smile, as he said, "Why yes, she will be at the Spice Islands when I get there. I often write to her." And his smile vanished.

Abe thought it was a strange response, but he liked this kid, and he had an idea. "What do you know about karma?" he asked.

Ray laughed and raised his hands. "Oh, I knew a Carmen in Odessa. She was a very nasty girl, and we had a great time together."

Abe laughed. "No. Not Carmen, karma. The Hindu or Buddhist concept of being rewarded for past deeds."

"Okay, I can dig that concept. Carmen really helped me out. Whew! She was a piece of work."

Abe laughed again and tried another tack, "What I'm saying is, I may be able to get you a job on a freighter out of Houston, headed for southeast Asia."

Ray was astounded — no more thoughts of Carmen. "What? How would I get on?"

"My cousin, Morris Klein, owns and operates a scrap metal freighter out of the Port of Houston, the motor vessel M/V Irony. The name shows he has a sense of humor. You may be able to get on as a cook, even though you are not an Able-Bodied Seaman. I can put in a call to him; I know he's in port, loading scrap metal. Are you interested?"

"Yes, I'm very interested," Ray said, "But you should tell the captain that I've never been at sea."

So possibly, with the help of good karma, memories of Carmen, and the goodwill of Abe Klein, Ray was closer to his dream than ever.

THEY ARRIVED IN DALLAS in the wee hours of morning and booked rooms on Harry Hines Boulevard, not far from where President Kennedy was assassinated. After catching up on sleep, Abe conducted business and dealt with authorities about his brother's death, and Ray cleaned up the car and did their laundry. They found a Cattleman's Steakhouse for dinner.

Abe had finished his meetings with the diamond trader and had called his cousin in Houston. Tomorrow, Ray would have an interview at the Anchor Tavern, in Humble Texas, for the position of cook on his cousin's freighter. A "Mr. Parker" would meet Ray there.

The next morning at 11:00 a.m., Abe and Ray were standing in front of a popcorn machine at the Dallas Bus Terminal, watching the big Greyhound buses coming and going.

"Ray, I can't thank you enough for helping me get to Dallas. The diamond deal is done. I will pick up my brother's remains for our trip home. Even though it's not conventional for traditional Jewish culture, his body was so damaged that we had him cremated — Ray, are you okay?"

Ray had blanched at the thought of burned remains, thinking of Giselle, burning up in the truck. He recovered, took a deep breath, and nodded yes.

Abe went on, "Here is the bus ticket I promised, plus $200 in appreciation of your help. Humble is near Houston, and the Anchor Tavern is a favorite local watering hole."

Ray settled in on the Greyhound bus for the four-hour trip, wondering about Mr. Parker. "You'll know him when you see him," he'd been told. What did that mean? He was to meet Mr. Parker at 5:00 p.m. *"Happy Hour,"* he thought.

Chapter 8
Cast of Characters

Humble was a small town thirty miles west of Houston. The Anchor Tavern was located in the heart of the city and was a lively place. Ray was early; he sat at the bar, people watching and listening to the locals. He noticed right away that Humble was pronounced "Umble" with a silent H. When he asked about it, the bartender said it was hard for Texans to say "Humble." Looking at the boisterous crowd, Ray could see there was no humility anywhere in the bar. As 5:00 p.m. neared, Ray speculated on what Mr. Parker would look like. How would Ray know him, a perfect stranger? As it turned out, there was no question at all.

The happy hour crowd was drifting in, two or three at a time, when Mr. Parker came through the door. Sure enough, Ray knew who he was. He was a world apart from the rest, looking like he belonged on a tramp freighter plowing through the South China Sea. He was small and scrawny, with bold-looking green eyes and a smooth hairless face, set off by a Māori chin tattoo that seemed to project out above a large Adam's apple. He was completely bald, not a hair anywhere, and wore a bright red do-rag that tailed down the back of his head. He had an imperial presence, the way he carried himself, like he owned the building, though he was only about five-foot four inches tall, and weighed about 120 pounds. The biggest surprise was when he spoke. He had the voice of a big man, a low bass and rumbling resonance, a shock coming from such a small guy.

Mr. Parker approached the bar, and spoke around the people crowded in front of him, who immediately moved aside, hearing the booming voice — only to see a runt with a red do-rag. His voice carried throughout the bar, causing people to pause and look up.

"Is there a Raymond Murphy in this bar?" he asked with a smile.

Incredibly, people started looking around for someone they couldn't know. *"The power of the voice,"* Ray thought. *"Should I salute, wave, genuflect? No, that wouldn't do."*

Instead, he raised his arm and smiled, "That would be me, Mr. Parker."

The two men moved to a small table near the back door, ordered beers and introduced themselves.

"My name is Clarence Parker," the small man said, "but I'm called Clink. You know the sound an empty wine bottle makes when it rolls out of your car door and hits the curb?"

Ray said, "Clink?"

"You got it in one," Clink said, "and you go by Ray, I'm guessing?"

"Yep," Ray answered, "Short and to the point."

"Okay, Ray, I'm interviewing you for the third cook's job on M/V Irony, right? I have only two questions. First, do you like to cook?"

"Yes, I do," said Ray.

"Okay. Second question. Tell me what would be in your favorite chili recipe."

Ray immediately rattled off the contents in a pot of chili he would make — beef or venison cubes, onions, garlic, tomatoes, his special blend of spices and chili powder, beer, etc. Clink grew very quiet, looked at him for a long moment. Ray thought, *"Oh boy, what have I missed? Have I flunked the test?"*

Clink slowly said, "What about beans? No beans in your chili?"

Ray swallowed. "No sir! I'm a Texan! I do like to experiment with spices in my chili, sometimes even add fresh chiles. But no beans. If it's got beans, it ain't chili. It's bean soup."

Clink leaned back, raised his hand in a salute and said, "Good. You're hired, if you can leave with us in a week or so. Let's get another beer."

THEY WERE JUST SETTLING in, thinking about ordering bar food, when the fight broke out. It was a mean fight, beer bottles and chairs flying, and it seemed to be spreading — suddenly, everyone was fighting. Clink and Ray were finishing their beers, looking at the back door, when sirens could be heard.

Clink said, "Maybe we should leave some shekels and make an exit out back. It's not our fight."

"Good idea," Ray said, dropping bills on the table and heading for the back door.

Too late. The police met them in the alley, and within the hour, they were being booked into jail for disturbing the peace.

As the deputy walked them back to their cell, Ray asked, "Where are all the other guys, the ones that were doing all the fighting?"

The deputy shook his head. "They were locals."

Ray asked, "No jail for locals?"

"Yep, they were locals," the deputy said again. Then he gave free advice. "The commode in the other cell is stopped up, so I have to put you two in with Junior. He's a big bully, but if you just accommodate him, let him do his thing, you should be okay."

Ray looked at Clink in disbelief, as the cell door closed behind them and the deputy scurried back down the hall. Junior was a big man, laying on the top bunk. He started issuing orders immediately.

"One of you sleeps on the floor, there's only two bunks in here. Don't flush the commode while I'm sleeping, and stay quiet as little mice, or I'll kick your ass! And what's that crap on your face, baldy?"

As Junior said this, he leaned forward to stare at them, his beady black eyes like buttons. He kept looking back at Ray, trying to stare him down. After a minute of staring, Ray slowly walked up to him, face to face. Then he reached up and grabbed Junior's ears in vise-like grips, and pulled him off the top bunk, Junior shouting, "Ow, ow, ow, ow," like a third grader being taken to the principal, as he hit the floor on his head. Being a big man, he took up a lot of space in the cell. Clink moved away from the action, starting to smile.

Junior rolled to come up fighting, but Ray was ready and gave him a tremendous kick in the solar plexus. Junior sagged, out of air, gripped his stomach and threw up. Ray moved around and kicked him again, this time very hard behind the ear, avoiding the temple. He thought it was nicely done.

Junior was finished. Down for the count. Ray rolled him over to the corner, through his own vomit, and asked Clink which bunk he wanted. Clink didn't say anything, just climbed onto the top bed.

As Ray crawled into the bottom bunk, he said, "I wish we'd had time to order that bar food, I'm hungry."

Clink finally spoke, with his deep voice. "Well, Ray, I can see you're not timid." He chuckled.

"I can't abide bullies." Ray said.

As they lay in the bunks in the dark, Clink said, "I saw you looking at my tattoo, let me tell you about it." He rolled sideways in the bunk. "In New Zealand I am best buds with a group of Māori's. You know, the natives. We partied together and I visited them and stayed with their families. They even told me, 'You can be one of us.' I thought no more about it until I woke up on a pool table in the back of an Irish bar called the Muddy Farmer in Auckland one morning. As I staggered to the head and washed my face, I saw the Māori chin tattoo for the first time. I hadn't felt a thing. Fortunately, my tattoo means 'Honored Guest.' It could have meant 'Slave Woman.'"

"Wow," Ray said with a smile, "That must have been one hell of a party."

Chapter 9
Sea Life: Aboard M/V Irony

At daylight the next morning, Clink felt a bump and looked down to see Ray helping Junior into the lower bunk. Junior was looking at Ray, trying to figure out what the hell happened. Three breakfast trays had been left just outside the bars. Ray wetted a napkin and gave it to Junior to wash his face.

Ray spoke in a low voice, "Junior, you shouldn't be trying to push people around, especially people you don't know, because you never know what might happen. It's like playing with a loaded gun. I know guys in the oil patch that would cut your throat in a heartbeat. So, think about it. Nobody likes a bully."

That said, Ray leaned forward and tapped Junior in the forehead, for emphasis.

Junior looked at him with big eyes and said, "I have a headache, and my ears hurt."

Mission done, Ray grabbed a piece of toast off one of the trays, looked up, smiled, and said, "Morning, Clink," like this was just another day at the office. "The good deputy left us some breakfast and hot coffee, would you like some?"

Clink smiled in appreciation of Ray's attitude. "Why yes, Ray. Thank you, coffee would be great, but we needn't bother with that jail food. Any minute, D-13, our First Mate, is going to be in here like a freight train, pissed off."

Ray nodded, puzzled. "Because they threw us in jail?"

"Not at all, my friend. He'll be pissed because you were supposed to cook his breakfast this morning aboard M/V Irony." Clink laughed. "Hell Ray, you're in trouble already and you haven't even started to work yet."

Clink eased off the top bunk, past a very quiet Junior, and said, "The D is gonna be hungry, so we'll be hunting up a big breakfast — he likes his breakfasts."

Ray was uneasy and wanted to know more about the First Mate, maybe better to defend himself. "His name is D-13?"

Clink smiled, "Demetrius Motchenbacher is his name. Counting the letters, D-13 works well for quick shipboard orders. He has his U.S. citizenship but he's from middle Europe somewhere, maybe Austria, won't say. For some unknown reason, he doesn't like Germans and won't have one on the boat."

AS IF ON CUE, A LOUD voice could be heard in the front office, moving their way.

D-13 was speaking like a machine gun, "... spoke to the bartender this morning, and he said my crew was nowhere near that little fight in the bar. And where are the real fighters? They tore that bar up, but none of them are in jail. Something stinks in this town. Have you ever heard of dungaree liberty? Our whole crew can come down here and ..."

"Okay, okay," the deputy said nervously, "Just get these two out of my jail. Look. They did something to Junior, look at him."

Junior was laying in the bunk, quiet, his eyes blinking. As the deputy opened the cell, the big First Mate was already introducing himself to Ray.

"Welcome aboard, Raymond. My name is Dimetrius Motchenbacher, I'm called D-13 or D. You're not related to that New Braunfels crowd, are you? It's full of Germans. Murphy is Irish, right? Goddamn, I can live with that."

D-13 stood six foot, six inches and weighed 250 pounds. His hands were huge and engulfed Ray's in the handshake.

"You were supposed to cook breakfast for me this morning, but I'll forgive you this one time." He laughed. "How'd you get him into all this trouble, Clink? Let's go get some breakfast, I'm starving, bet you are too."

They found a Pancake House, had huge breakfasts, and were touring the ship by noon, meeting the crew and inspecting the galley. Ray loved the galley, with its huge diesel stove, a walk-in reefer, and separate pantry. Pots and pans hanging, swaying with the movement of the ship. Adjacent to the galley was the ship's table with bench seating for twelve, like the Apostles. Ray could see himself serving up meals and bullshitting with the crew. It would be fun. Like most chefs, Ray wanted to be close to his customers to get their feedback. He envisioned many happy hours, sitting with the crew and swapping stories, a favorite pastime.

CLINK INTRODUCED RAY to his "bunkies" in the crew's quarters, a big Samoan ABS (Able-Bodied Seaman) called Tiny (just Tiny), and the ship's machinist, Finas Blankenship. First Mate D-13 found them and took Ray to meet Captain Klein in his quarters adjacent to the wheelhouse. Outside the door, they shook hands and D-13 departed. Ray didn't know ship protocol, didn't know if he should salute or not, so he just stood there.

"Ray, I understand you helped Abe out, and you've done some cooking," Morris Klein said. Morris was a rotund version of his cousin Abe.

"I was a short-order cook for a diner," Ray answered. He didn't appreciate the term "done some cooking."

Morris picked up on Ray's disapproval, "You must understand, Ray, that you will be on trial here, as we will be at sea for a long time with the crew we have, and can't change them mid-ocean."

Ray gave the captain an even look. "Let the trial begin, Captain. You should know if I pack the gear well before the ship departs."

Ray continued to look at the captain, until Morris said, "Very well, then, talk to D about the provisioning list."

Ray said, "Okay," turned and left, closing the door behind him without another word.

Morris looked at the closed door and said to himself, "Well, it seems I've pissed off our new cook. I hope he's not too high strung, with the bunkie's he has. Maybe I should get D-13 to explain the lay of the land down in the crew's quarters."

The next morning, Ray was in the First Mate's quarters getting instructions.

"Here is the provisioning list for three months at sea. As you can see, we feed the crew well. Many of the vendors will deliver to dockside, but some goods you need to pick up with the ship's leased truck. It's all there on the list. Being a cook, you might enjoy Houston's markets. Here's the truck keys and some cash. Watch your back on the waterfront, and don't forget to get receipts."

D-13 slowed his rapid-fire talk, and motioned Ray to a chair. "Before you go, I've been asked to tell you a little about your bunkie's. Tiny, the big Samoan, is a little pushy, but he's okay. Finas is another story. He's a great machinist, so we keep him on. But he came back from Vietnam with a Silver Star and a stutter. But more than that, he has an edge about him, like you don't know what he's going to do, especially if you know his history."

"Finas was a forward observer for the Seventh Marines, on a hill calling in artillery and air strikes," said D-13. "The North Vietnamese Army sent infantry to knock his position out. Then they sent mortars, then infantry again. When a Marine Rifle Company secured the hill two days later, they found Finas covered in blood from hand-to-hand combat, with knives and guns strapped all over him, stuttering and shooting at the departing NVA. There were about thirty dead around the post. He was rotated back to his outfit, but was too scary even for the Marine vets, so they gave him the Silver Star and sent him home." D-13 shook his head and continued.

"Now, when Finas thinks someone is out of line, he sits very close to them, looks them in the eye, and starts stuttering, and says he wants to talk about God and Country. It scares the hell out of everyone. And he has this unnerving habit of talking to himself."

D-13 leaned back and smiled, "So that's your other bunkie, Finas. Interesting, eh? Have fun in town. It's a great city."

Ray shook his head as he walked down the gangplank to the truck. "Jesus, what a bunch of characters. It's going to be quite a trip."

Ray spent the day in the stores of Houston, religiously following the shopping list. Buying for eighteen for three months was a new experience, he was glad to have the detailed list. When he found the Houston spice markets, he started talking to Giselle, imagining her alongside as he rummaged through an amazing array of spices. With a shrug, he started buying spices not on the shopping list, hoping the Captain would be as forgiving as Wesley Shaw was. He might be forgiven, if he didn't get fired first. Ray grew philosophical about getting fired as he drove back to the ship. From his experience, after getting fired, or getting your ass kicked often enough, you just didn't worry about it anymore.

SMEDLEY JONES, THE first shift cook who had been on leave, met Ray at the gangplank to help load provisions. He was a cheerful fellow from Louisiana, and spoke with a Cajun accent, slaughtering the "r's." '

"Hey Ray, heard all about you already. You a short order cook, eh? Glad to have you on board. Did my twenty with the Navy, but can't stay off the ships."

"You were a cook the whole time?"

"Yep, cooked the whole time and saw the world, too."

Ray was intrigued. "Did you spend much time in Indonesia? Have you heard of the Spice Islands?"

"Oh yeah, the Navy did fleet maneuvers there, had to keep an eye on the wily Chinese." Smedley said. "I'll tell you about the islands, and them big motherfucking Komodo lizards, too. They'll scare the hell outa you."

Ray was encouraged. Smedley knew about the Spice Islands. Like RD always said, luck is where you find it. Provisioning done, and with Smedley cooking, Ray started a batch of his "Odessa-Famous" hot sauce. Afterwards, he had free time to roam the ship.

He liked the open decks and the stern deck with awning covers for lounging, the warm passageways and the view from the wheelhouse. He found the ship's library, was impressed by the engine room and inspected the deck cranes with professional interest. To Ray, the ship felt like a cozy and compact living and working quarters — where you could hang out with comfort and feel at home. "*This should be easy,*" he thought, "*I haven't even seen any roaches.*"

Then Clink got a message that changed things.

It was 4:00 a.m. on a Sunday and most of the crew were ashore. Smedley and Ray were preparing breakfasts for early risers and Clink Parker was sitting at the table lamenting a message from his kid sister.

"Sherry's done it again," he was whining, "Another move with that goddamn piano. She's driving me to drink."

Ray was amused, never having seen the ever-poised Clink stirred up. "She wants you to move her piano?" He could hear Smedley laughing from the galley.

"Not just any piano, a concert grand piano, weighs in at 1,100 pounds."

"Can't she hire it done?" Ray asked.

Clink shook his head, "Not Sherry. You gotta understand, she does everything her own way. Look at her 'employment' for example. She does real estate appraisals for mortgage companies. Good at it. Can do three appraisals a day with her two girls in tow. They picnic on the lawn or in the car, while she whips out the appraisals, making about $600 a day. She makes more money than Morris, working part time. And she moves a lot, with that piano. Puts it in the front room with a candle on it, and can't play it for shit."

Clink started counting with his fingers. "Let's see, I've moved her from Cut and Shoot to Lampasas, then over to Dime Box. Now she wants to move to Midlothian, up past Waxahachie — and she knows I'll do it if I can. She's my baby sister and I'll do anything for her, but we got three trucks of scrap coming in tomorrow, and I gotta load."

Ray grinned and lifted his coffee cup. "Don't want to keep you from that piano. How about I load for you tomorrow?"

"You can run a crane?" Clink asked.

"Yup. I was looking at your crane the other day, it's a modified Bucyrus Erie cable rig like we had in the oil patch, no problem."

So Clink got to move Sherry's piano again, and Ray began operating the crane, as well as cooking aboard M/V Irony.

Chapter 10
The Voyage

Clarence (Clink) Parker was back aboard the ship the next Monday, having taken a week off. It took four days to move the piano, and Ray was doing fine with the crane work, so Clink spent some time with his family. Now he was in the captain's quarters, reporting in with Morris and D-13, to see how things were going. They were sitting on wicker chairs, drinking coffee. The ship was rolling slightly with the morning tide, and busy harbor sounds could be heard through open port holes. The odor of saltwater and diesel blended with the coffee. As longtime seamen, they took little notice of it.

The First Mate was going over details, "The crew is at full strength and healthy, all have current passports and are properly vaccinated. The ship is in trim, as loaded, both fore and aft, and port and starboard. The scrap metal has settled evenly in the holds — Murphy is an artist with the crane, Clink. He back sticked the metal into the corners like you do. Says he learned it putting drill stems in wellheads. So, we've got enough room above the metal for high volume, low weight cargo in Honduras, when we've burned off fuel and can stay under the Plimsoll lines. More cargo, more money for ship and crew," D-13 said, as he took a breath and drank more coffee. (Plimsoll lines are the stability marks on a ship's hull).

Morris was nodding his head, pleased.

"How's Ray doing otherwise?" Clink asked. "Is he going to make the grade?"

"Oh, yeah." Morris said. "He's a good addition to the crew. He's very curious, roams all over the ship, asks a million questions. And he's a good cook. Have you tried his hot sauce?"

D-13 said, "We had a squall come through here, and Ray got seasick with the ship tied to the dock. It was hilarious, and he took the crew's harassment well. Hope he does okay at sea."

Clink could tell they were taken with Ray, the way they told the stories.

D-13 went on, "In the crew's quarters, Ray already got in a fight with Tiny, bit off a chunk of his ear. Then they went to the ship's infirmary, and both sewed the chunk back on. By 2:00 a.m., with a bottle of scotch, they became the best of buddies." He laughed, "Tiny's ear is a little crooked, though."

Clink chuckled, "He goes for the ears, don't he?"

D-13 added, "He's settling in as a cook, wears an apron that says Spice Hound, and does some experiments with spices. He got the carpenter, Chips, to make a spice rack, and found a huge coffee urn at a waterfront pawn shop for the galley."

ON THIS SAME MORNING, one deck below, Ray was in the ship's library, working on his novel. He noticed other crew writing letters home before the ship's departure. He thought, *"Good idea,"* and wrote notes to Miss Teel, RD, and the diner crew. Then he started writing to Giselle, and it felt really good to put his thoughts about her in writing. He told her how much he missed her, described the trip from Odessa to Houston, and said that he was headed to the Spice Islands, like they had dreamed. After much thought, he included the St. Christophers medal in the packet to be mailed. It had been found in Giselle's belongings left at the funeral home, not included in the shipment to France because it was scorched and bent. Ray didn't feel right keeping it. He still had the Paris address.

That evening there was a party on the fantail, under the awnings. Food and drink, courtesy of the captain, following his reading of the ship's orders for the upcoming voyage. The ship would proceed from Houston to Honduras, Panama, the Hawaiian Islands, Hong Kong, then to the Zongheng Iron and Steel plant in Hebei province, China.

Smedley and Ray finished their cooking duties and joined the party. Clink was holding court, telling about the Māori, the discussion brought on, no doubt, by his chin tattoo.

"You know, they were originally from the Cook Islands. They left Rarotonga in the Southern Cooks, about 800 years ago. They took fourteen huge outriggers, bound for New Zealand. Only seven outriggers made it," Clink said.

"How did they know about New Zealand?" Ray asked.

"They could tell by the clouds. The Māori name for New Zealand is the 'Land of the Long White Cloud.'" Clink chuckled, "Of course, nowadays, the Australians, ever New Zealand's competitor in sports, call it the 'Land of the Wrong White Crowd.'"

After the laughter died down, he continued, "The Māori had the islands to themselves for a long time; and ate the first white men that arrived. Then the English came and the 'civilizing' began."

It was a good story. They partied into the night.

The M/V Irony departed the Port of Houston at dawn the next day, bound for Honduras, a five-day voyage. For three of these days, Ray was so seasick he begged the crew to put him out of his misery, and had trouble working his shifts. He vowed to leave the ship in Honduras, to go back to Odessa. However, as they approached Honduras, he felt well enough to become curious enough to ask about the cargo to be loaded on there.

"Hammocks" Clink said, "Thousands of hand-made hammocks. They like hammocks here, string them around the open air bars, so you can drink your fill, then flop over into a hammock. We'll be taking a load of them to Hawaii."

"I'd like to experience that," Ray said with a grin.

"Oh, you will," Clink answered, seeing that Ray was going to be okay.

Sure enough, Ray and Finas Blankenship ended up in an open-air bar, drinking tropical fruit drinks, looking at the hammocks.

"We're not ready for that yet, have another drink," Finas said with a stutter.

Later in the evening, after many more drinks, the two were laying in hammocks in the humid sunset.

Ray asked, "Finas, I don't want to offend you, but why to do talk to yourself?"

Finas looked at the drink resting on his chest, and said, "I'm talking to the ghosts that I see every day and night. Some I've killed, some were friends killed near me. It helps me to talk to them."

Ray was quiet for a while, then said," I have a ghost that I think about a lot."

Finas nodded and grinned, unusual for him, and said "Try talking to your ghost, it will help."

Ten days later their ship was entering the Panama Canal, after a five-day passage from Honduras and five days of getting provisions in Colon and waiting to enter the locks. Ray was enchanted by the jungle they passed through and the toucans flying overhead, beaks down. A loud, low-pitched scream pierced the air, and Ray almost dropped a tray of enchiladas he was serving on the back deck.

"Holy shit!" he stammered, "What was that?"

The veteran crew laughed, and Morris said, "Howler monkey, would you believe?"

Smedley said, "Can you imagine what Vasco Balboa and his troops thought when they first heard that? Sounds like the hubs of hell, and it's a little monkey about two feet high."

As they exited the canal, service boats delivered more Balboa beer and provisions to the crew, paid for with Balboas (U.S. currency, called Balboas in Panama). Ray handed the provisioning crew a handful of letters and a couple of bucks for postage.

M/V Irony made a forty-two-day passage to Hong Kong, with a stop in Hawaii to offload the hammocks. During the voyage, Ray grew comfortable on the ocean and became a good crewman, even in rough weather.

In his spare time, he wrote another letter to Giselle, outlining his adventures from Panama to Hawaii and beyond, and describing the crew, the landscapes and the countries he had seen. He had developed a new sauce recipe from the flavors experienced in central America, and he shared it in his letter. The letter writing was therapeutic for Ray, helping ease his broken heart. He also wrote short notes to Miss Teel and RD, and hoped he would be able to send them sometime during his trip. In Hawaii, he asked one of the loaders to mail the letters for him.

On the passage from Hawaii to Hong Kong, Ray had lots of spare time to continue his writing. He started another novel, this one full of the characters he had met along the way, and wrote another letter to Giselle, describing life aboard, the sights and sounds of the sea, and his adventures with the crewmen. He was fascinated with the ever-changing ocean and skies, the bioluminescence in the dark nights, the sea life; dolphins, sharks, whales and birds. Everything was so different from Odessa.

Ray was excited about getting closer to southeast Asia and the Spice Islands. As they prepared meals, he badgered Smedley to describe the Spice Islands, with unending curiosity.

"Ray, I didn't live there or anything! We just stopped by on our way between bases. It was hot, humid and beautiful, but so are a lot of the islands."

AT ONE POINT, THE FREIGHTER suddenly stopped. The quiet was amazing, and they drifted with the currents as Finas dove deep into the mechanical room and banged on the engine. Ray enjoyed this time, sitting on deck and watching the dolphins and albatrosses, laughing to himself about how these swells would have made him seasick just a few weeks ago. Finally, they were underway again. But as they approached Hong Kong harbor, Morris called the crew together for the bad news.

"Gentlemen, we've got major engine problems and will be in Hong Kong for months, getting repairs after we offload our cargo. Finas did a great job jury rigging a fix, but it won't get us all the way to the plant and back, so it'll be shipped over land from here. In two weeks, you will be 'on the beach' in Hong Kong, with a small bonus. Sorry about that."

Ray sat at the galley table thinking about being "on the beach." Unemployed in Hong Kong. What would he do? How was he going to get to Indonesia to see the Spice Islands? Maybe by airplane?

Then Clink had a request. "Hey Ray, want to help me inventory our return cargo, for when and if we ever get this engine fixed? It's in a warehouse over on B dock."

"Be glad to, Clink. I've finished my cooking shift."

THE WAREHOUSE CARGO was a surprise, with Chinese motorcycles to be exported to America. Ray was enthralled — flat track motorcycle racing was popular in Odessa. He looked one over, a 750 cc Yang Tse model. It looked very sturdy. Then he looked up toward the other end of the warehouse and saw Giselle. He was shocked, speechless, and staggered toward her, his heart in his mouth. Closer, he saw it wasn't Giselle, but a smaller version of her, with the same red hair coiled down her front, fair skin with freckles, and, Mother of God, the same green eyes. He stood in front of her, staring, until she introduced herself with a Scottish accent.

"Hello, I'm Ginger McGregor, here with my husband to pick up a motorcycle." She pointed daintily over her shoulder, "Angus is round the corner, taking care of details."

She spoke with an enchanting lilt. Ray was standing there stammering, when Clink showed up and smoothly introduced Ray to Ginger. He asked Ginger about their plans with the motorcycles.

Ginger smiled, showing brilliant white teeth, "Oh, we are touring on bikes again. We've done South Africa, now we want to take a shot at China."

Angus, a tall, lanky man, showed up and introduced himself. He also had flaming red hair plus a huge moustache. Ray imagined him in a kilt, doing a sword dance.

"We're looking at the bike to see if it's big enough for the two of us. We crossed South Africa that way on a BMW, but it was a little larger. With Ginger's small size, we may be able to do a China trip with backpacks, at the cost of being a wee bit top-heavy. However, we may need to strap on panniers to move the weight lower, aye?"

As the discussion went on, Ray couldn't take his eyes off Ginger. She looked so much like Giselle, he couldn't believe it. He heard Clink ask which way they were going.

"West, then southwest, toward Thailand," Angus said.

Ray finally found his voice, "Wait. Toward Indonesia?"

Before the day was out, Ray had purchased a Chinese motorcycle too, and Angus and Ginger had invited him to join them on their journey across southwestern China. Their roughly planned route would take them along the roads bordering the Xun Jiang (Pearl) River out of Hong Kong, hook up with back roads to travel along the Pearl to the mighty Yangtze, then on to a network of rivers and roads leading to the Mekong, through Thailand and Malaysia, getting Ray close to Indonesia.

Ray invited Angus and Ginger back to the ship and cooked dinner for them. They sat at the galley table and discussed the adventure.

"Why do you want to go to Indonesia?" Angus asked.

Ray grinned as he served up more stew, "I'm really into spices, and in Odessa I met a remarkable French chef. She and I shared a dream of seeing the Spice Islands in Indonesia. She's gone now, but I still have the dream and I aim to see the Spice Islands in her memory. She looked a lot like you, Ginger, so forgive me if I stare at you occasionally. I miss her."

Embarrassed a little, Ray changed the subject. "How long have you'all been traveling?"

Ginger answered, with her beautiful lilting brogue, "For a while, every chance we get. I'm a nurse and work long hours to get traveling time off, and Angus has a construction company with a very good foreman, so we have time for travel adventures."

Angus added, "We live in Dundee, northeast Scotland, on the edge of the North Sea, so we enjoy these lower latitude adventures. My grandfather had been in China during the Great War, and afterwards, traveled to a place called Guigang, on the Pearl River. I'd like to see it, he told me it was beautiful, filled with lotus flowers, and very historical. The start of the Silk Road."

"And we want to see the Yangtze River, but avoid most of the big cities and the traffic," added Ginger. "There's usually good camping and friendly villages along the waterways."

The trio spent a week learning and tuning up the bikes, getting tool kits, saddlebags, backpacks and provisions. They toiled for hours over maps of the route, which were inadequate. They would head north out of Hong Kong, following the Pearl River as it turned westerly. The route would be through cities initially, then it looked like they would travel into more rural areas before reaching Guigang. There was a lot they didn't know.

When he wasn't helping to offload the ship, Ray visited markets in Hong Kong and discovered Chinese tea houses and apothecaries, with their full drawers of herbs, spices, and other raw materials for teas, health potions and Chinese medicines. *"Giselle would love this,"* Ray thought as he roamed, tasted, and soaked up the different culture.

Finally, a going-away party was held on the fantail of M/V Irony, with steak and lobster and Tsingtao Chinese beer.

"When you get to Singapore," Clink said, "I'll meet you at the Raffles Hotel, home of the world-famous Singapore Sling."

"You're on," Ray laughed, thinking, *"I don't know about Raffles, but I'll find it."*

Ray was given going-away gifts by the crew; a hand-held compass "to help him find his way" and a money belt for bail, to keep him out of jail.

"How many times have you been in jail, Ray?" one of the crew asked.

Ray laughed, and said, "I'll have to plead the fifth on that."

It was a good party. Ray said his goodbyes to his shipmates, joined the McGregors and they were ready to go.

The last evening aboard the ship, Ray wrote a letter to Giselle, to go out with the mail. He described his latest adventures, the Chinese foods, herbs and spices, the new friends he'd made. He outlined their planned route across part of China and along the Mekong River. He told her again how he loved her and dreamed of seeing the Spice Islands with her. Mailing her the letters made him feel like she was still with him and would meet him there.

Chapter 11
Motorcycles and the Trial

On the road, the view from their motorcycles was a revelation for Ray. He was new to China, and marveled at the river-based life and traffic. Junks, sampans, Indonesian freighters and small river boats were scattered along the banks. There were cooking fires and colorful laundry flying like flags. Floating vendors sold food, flowers, chickens, fruits and vegetables, pigs, pastries and more. The air was warm and heavy with the heat and fragrance of tropical flowers. For Ray, compared to the flat desert of Odessa, it was an enchanting place.

He followed behind Angus and Ginger, giving them space, because he didn't want them to regret including him on their trip, and besides, he enjoyed looking at Ginger's cute little backside, it reminded him of Giselle. Outside the city, the road was rough, strewn with rocks, with deep ruts and potholes. A blanket of dust covered everything, making visibility limited and breathing difficult. By late afternoon they were parked under a banyan tree, seeking shelter from a tropical downpour, rain like Ray had never seen. They'd strung a canvas cover to stop the drips and were checking out their gear and the bikes.

"This rain will pass, and we can make the next village before nightfall," Angus said, looking at the map.

"Sounds good, I'll clean the carburetor air intake screens," Ray said. "Did you see rain like this in South Africa?"

"Not even close, and now the dust is mud," Ginger said.

They rode on, and the clay was very slick, causing Angus to lose control and skid the bike about twenty feet on its side — nobody hurt.

"We are too top heavy with this camping gear on back," he complained.

"Why don't I carry some of your gear?" Ray offered.

"No, we need to be able to handle all of our gear, or get rid of it," Angus said, and Ginger nodded.

They pushed on and made the village by nightfall, found lodging, and a noodle cafe. It had been a long first day. The next day, the weather and road improved and the trio rode into Guigang early enough to tour the city, which was full of lotus gardens and pagodas. The port area was busy with ships, and they found a restaurant serving seafoods they had never seen before. Ginger made Angus and Ray try everything, much to the amusement of the staff and other customers.

From Guigang, they rode steadily for ten days, alternating between camping and village lodging, depending on availability. Angus and Ginger were good traveling companions, stopping often to stretch their legs, and flexible in the route, sights and experiences. They saw amazing countryside, intriguing villages and ornate temples. They tried lots of new foods; one of Ray's favorites were buns cooked in pottery ovens, they reminded him of Texas yeast rolls. They got advice from people they met, often using sign language and gestures, to find their way to the Yangtze, and followed the river upstream. After a very rough section of road, they came to a nice-looking village and decided to rest for a few days. They arrived just in time for the excitement.

"YOU HERE FOR THE TRIAL?" the tall, bearded Australian asked as they bellied up to his bar, an establishment they were astonished to find in the small Chinese village.

"Just passing through," Angus said. "What brought you here?"

"My wife, mate. Crazy about her, so I followed her home." He laughed. "My name's Graham, you can call me Gray. You ought to witness the trial, long as you're here. It's going to be most unusual."

"How so?" Ray asked, ever curious.

Gray explained, "He's called Fredric the Great, because he's big, you see. Stays here in the village when he's not working down in Thailand. What happened was, Fred, we call him Fred, was hanging out up by the main road when two Germans started tormenting him. He took it for as long as he could, then turned on them and killed them. There were witnesses."

Gray opened another beer. Apparently, he was his own best customer. "The Magistrate then sent out a squad to execute Fred, but the whole village started protesting. So, the Magistrate ordered a trial, which starts tomorrow morning. Everybody's invited."

Ginger was astonished, "They were going to execute this guy without a trial?"

"Oh love," Gray said, "Did I forget to mention that Fred is an elephant? He logs teak in Thailand when he's not up here with his owner in the off season. The locals love him. He's very gentle, likes the kids. He kneels down to give them rides. No way he'd hurt anyone unless provoked."

Later, they discussed Graham's journey to China. In the Australian army, he'd been in "Languages," posted to the Defense Language Institute in Monterey, California, to learn Chinese. While on duty at the Australian Consulate in Hong Kong, he'd met his wife. She was from the village, but was working in Hong Kong as an interpreter. They worked together for years before their "retirement." Graham didn't retire well, so he started the bar to keep out of trouble.

"When you've settled in, come to the trial. It's being held in a field, with bleachers, across the way."

Angus, Ginger and Ray found decent rooms near the bar and cleaned up, blessed relief from days on the trail. Ray heard Angus and Ginger making love in their room and envied them. He couldn't help feeling strongly toward Ginger, she was so much like Giselle. He knew it was wrong, but felt he loved her, a little bit.

Gray, wearing his outback hat, met them at breakfast at their inn and offered to accompany them to the trial. Because he was a nice guy and so insistent, they agreed.

As they headed out, Gray pointed out the trial situation. "You see that big hole by the bleachers? That was to be Fred's grave. Humane, eh?"

The big elephant was staked, the hole immediately behind him, with seats in a semicircle around the front. The jurors, half of them soldiers, the other half village folk, were in raised bleachers, looking down on the proceedings, but still looking up at the elephant. In front of the jury, two tables were for prosecution and defense. The judge maintained order from a pulpit facing Fred. Many of the gallery seats were close to the elephant.

Gray explained the set-up, "Bloody hell, the audience gallery is arranged close to Fred, in hopes he will get excited, hurt someone, and make their case."

The prosecutor was an army captain with a shaved head, shiny riding boots and an arrogant, condescending attitude, like he was above all this circus. He stood, and almost clicked his heels. Astonishingly, he wore riding spurs, like he'd just dismounted from a polo pony. Gray translated as the prosecutor spoke.

"This animal killed two German tourists, by sitting on them. This elephant is very fast, unpredictable, and could kill anyone in this gallery at any time." he bellowed, as he paced back and forth.

Some in the gallery, very close to Fred, looked at him fearfully. Fredric the Great looked down on them with placid eyes, very calm, like he was taking in the argument. On the very front row sat Angus, Ginger and Ray, with Gray sitting behind them, looking up at the magnificent beast in wonderment.

The captain went on, pointing at the elephant, "This animal may have a thirst for killing now, and could rampage through the village, causing untold harm." After more loud rhetoric in the same vein, the prosecution recommended the death penalty and rested its case.

The defense took the floor (or field, in this case). The elephant handler, called a mahout, was a small, delicate Indian named Meshri. He spoke with a refreshing economy of words in a melodic, low voice that carried well, and was the opposite of the captain's angry yelling. He looked at the jury steadily.

"I am Fredric's handler. We log teak together in the highlands. It is hard, brutal work. You can see the scars on my elephant. Limbs break and slash across us. You can see my scars, too, like my elephant's. In all the time we've worked together, I have never once seen my elephant angry or violent. Frederic is a docile, beautiful animal. He was driven to extremes by drunken Germans, who were yelling, poking and slashing him with their hiking sticks. They jabbed him in unmentionable places, shouted, hit and kicked at him. He was chained, as is required for unattended elephants, while undergoing this torture, so he did what he could. He sat on them, with no intention of harm, but merely to stop their torture. My elephant is a gentle creature. He deserves to go free."

During Meshri's eloquent speech, Ginger sat on the front row looking into Fred's eyes. She was intent and was leaning forward, with hair coiled down her front. As if on cue, when Meshri said "My elephant is a gentle creature . . ." Fred's trunk slowly moved toward Ginger, and gently moved her hair back up over her shoulder, out of her eyes. While doing this, Fred looked steadily into Ginger's eyes. It was a beautiful gesture.

The elephant was acquitted; and given early retirement to stay in the village. No more logging. The village celebrated.

AFTER THE TRIAL, GINGER, Angus and Ray met with Gray at his bar for dinner. They discussed the next leg of their journey.

Gray was worried, "Mates, I have to tell you, the road from here gets more treacherous in a number of ways."

He had the full attention of the traveling trio. Information on this part of the route had been sketchy. It was a remote area.

"To start with, the road itself is like an obstacle course," Gray said. "You have pockets of soft clay that will mire your bikes down. Bloody hell, I've gotten stuck on that road many times with my truck! Then you have rocks and washouts to deal with — but the worst hazard, I have to tell you, are the cats."

They peered at him in disbelief, "Did you say cats?" Angus said.

"Yes, two big freaking rogue tigers that have developed an appetite for human flesh, and can easily run travelers down." Gray sipped his beer and nodded, "Tigers usually hunt alone, but these beauties have partnered up to be a killing combination. They've taken many travelers along that road. You will see groups of walkers on the road wearing face masks on the back of their head, turned around, in the belief that the cats won't jump them with a 'face' looking at them. The tigers usually attack from behind."

Ginger put her fork down and quit eating her dinner. "Is it possible to outrun the cats with our motorcycles?"

Gray raised his hands, palms out. "I would say yeah, if the road's not too rough, and you don't dump the bikes in that slick clay. Best to give the road some time between rains."

Angus and Ray looked at each other, eyes wide.

"Blimy, who would have thought we'd be dodging tigers on this bloody road?" Angus said. "How fast can a tiger run?"

"They can be very fast," Gray said. "I heard about hunters going into the bush to kill a tiger, wearing armor-type protection, and by the time they got the cat, it had gotten a piece of all of them — they are that fast.

"Are there any other routes?" Ray asked.

"Not unless you want to go backwards and around," said Gray. "You can travel via the main roads through Vietnam."

"What should we do?" Ray asked.

Angus and Ginger looked at each other, then nodded in unison. Angus said, "We really want to do this trip. Why don't we wait for the road to dry a bit, then make a run for it?"

Ray smiled, "I can see you two are really caught up in this adventure. I'll go over the bikes while we wait. I don't want to get 'et by a big cat on a muddy road in China."

They waited for three days, touring the village, stopping by to see Fredric the elephant, and visiting with Gray at the bar every night. The road was drying out. Ray cleaned and tuned up the motorcycles, then organized their packs for a quick release, with a line to cut to drop the load if a cat got too close. He showed it to Angus.

"You just cut this line, it's laced to the others, and the pack drops off as Ginger moves up. Think it'll work?"

Angus fingered the line. "Aye, should work quickly if you have a handy belt knife to reach it, and I see you don't have one. Here, take mine. I have another one in my other pack."

Ray thanked Angus for the knife and did a trial run, cut the line and dumped the packs. It worked fine.

Ginger came around the corner. "Hey guys, I have an idea. Why don't we take some bait to drop for the cats if they are following us?"

They discussed the idea with Gray, who said "I don't think it would work. In fact, it might attract them, and if it stopped the first cat, would the other cat stop, too?"

In the end, they abandoned the idea. No bait. They used the time to write letters home. Ray sent another to Giselle, describing the trip so far. He knew she wasn't there, but it felt good to write. Being around Ginger, the Giselle-look-alike, was uplifting and depressing at the same time. The mixed emotions were confusing to him. He dreamed of Giselle often.

GRAY ORGANIZED A NIGHT out at a karaoke bar. It was set up with a sound system and lyric screens for the singers. Karaoke was very popular, and locals would stand at the mike, look at the song's words on the screen and belt out popular songs in English.

Ray asked Gray, "Why do so many speak English here?"

Gray blinked and tossed down a shot. He was drinking boilermakers. "It's the karaoke, and the bloody missionaries. They are all over the place — Catholics, Baptists, Methodists, Presbyterians, the bloody lot. If you are not careful, you'll be doing Mass, or getting baptized in the river, or planting vegetables in their garden and wearing long hot clothes to cover up your sinful body. Bloody hell, it's grown hard to nail any pussy around here, from all these virtuous women." Gray looked at Ginger, "Oops, sorry love, I've had too many boilermakers."

They all laughed. Later in the evening, Ginger was persuaded to the mike, where she sang "Morning Train" with such feeling that Ray was almost overcome with emotion, thinking of Giselle. It was a great party until the big, bald, tattooed Dutchman arrived.

Gray almost flinched when the big Dutchman walked in and sat at a table across from them, and stared around the room. Gray told about him in a low voice, "That bloke comes here quite often on some kind of business, won't say what. Likes to harass the karaoke singers. He's an arrogant, snide, bully."

As he said this, Ray shook his head, like, here we go again. The man was huge, with prison tattoos all over, and projected a mean sneer toward everybody. Right away, he started loudly harassing the karaoke singers.

"You call that singing?" he called out in a loud deep voice. Or, "Quit stuttering, you're spitting into the mike," he taunted, destroying the pleasant evening. Then the big Dutchman saw Ginger, and was apparently taken by her beauty.

"Now there's a nice little piece I would like to make sing," he said with a nasty laugh. "Why don't you lose those fairies, and join me for dinner?"

As he said this, Ray started bending his dinner fork handle and curling it back to rest on his palm, with the tangs pointing out. Some of the customers were leaving.

Angus was getting up when Ray interrupted, calling out, "Hey fat man, why don't you settle down?"

The Dutchman arrogantly strode across the room to take on Angus, who was ready to fight this monster, standing up and raising his hands. But as the Dutchman got close, Ray stepped in and drove the fork into his midsection. The bent handle protruded from the man's stomach like an obscene decoration. Blood started gushing around it, as the giant looked down and started squealing in disbelief. By then, Ray was winding up with a great roundhouse swing, driving Gray's nice, heavy boilermaker beer mug into the side of the Dutchman's head — beer, scotch and shotglass flying. The man went down in a heap, out cold.

Ray apologized to Gray in a normal voice, "Sorry about your drink, Gray, I'll buy you another one." Then he looked down and said, "Dang, I got beer all over my clean clothes."

The bar was quiet.

Gray sighed, "Maybe we should call it an evening."

As they left the bar, Ray said, "He sure did squeal, didn't he?" Walking down the street, Ray started singing, "My baby takes the morning train...."

Chapter 12
A Bad Road and the Cats

With the roads drying and a fair weather outlook, Angus, Ginger and Ray huddled over the maps for what seemed like the hundredth time. Even with Grays notes, the maps were still poor and they were concerned about the route.

Gray was giving them assurances, "It's some beautiful country, but with mountainous canyons and jungle. Generally, your path will be toward the southwest, until you reach the Mekong River watershed. The Mekong runs from China through Laos, Thailand and Cambodia and Vietnam, through the Mekong Delta to the South China Sea. You can cut across Thailand, down the peninsula to Malaysia, and on to Singapore — then for Ray, from there it's a boat ride to Indonesia. Piece of cake!"

Ginger laughed and Angus asked, "Except for the tigers that might eat us, what else do we need to worry about, besides getting lost, flats or breakdowns?"

Gray looked at the ceiling and scratched his chin. "Well, there are river pirates that ply the Mekong in armed junks. The river villages pay 'tribute' for their protection. They control different sections of the river and sometimes war on each other."

"Are you serious?" Angus asked. "This is 1990!"

"Yes, but these are very remote areas, and they actually do the villages some good."

Ray shook his head, "Man, I'm a long way from Odessa."

They laughed.

THE TRIO DEPARTED THE next morning, after saying goodbyes to village friends, and Frederic and Gray. The road was dry and in fair condition, the motorcycles were running smoothly, and they were in great spirits. They made good time on the road for eight days as the route was curving more southwest. Ray, Angus and Ginger were good travel companions, with complementary skills, and similar travel styles, adventurous spirits, humor and curiosity.

The terrain went from mountainous to warmer and more marshy, and the jungle grew thicker. Every now and then they passed villages and small temples, all ornate and well kept. They stopped often to tour sites, eat, stretch their legs and discuss their progress. The industrious Chinese had "petrol stations" even in the remote areas, selling fuel in liter soda bottles for their motorcycles.

As they fueled up at one such station, an elderly man wearing a coolie hat spoke to them in broken English, "Your motorbikes fast, yes?"

Angus smiled, "Yes, on a good road."

The man pointed down the road and said, "Near here, they make sport to chase down motorbikes."

"Who makes sport?" asked Ray.

"The cats. Very, very fast." The man shook his head and looked at Ginger.

"I wonder how much trouble we are in," Ray said, to no one in particular.

A few miles down the road, they started riding past small groups of people on the trail wearing masks of faces on the backs of their heads, hurrying along the road, looking terrified.

Angus slowed down so he could talk to Ray. "We may be in a shitload of trouble."

Ray thought, *"Shitload, isn't that an American term?"*

Angus signaled to pull over. "What do you think?"

Ray looked back at the jungle they'd passed. "Man, I don't know. The cats might be behind us. How do we know?"

Ginger was looking at the topo map. "The ground may be rising in front of us, roads not so slick, maybe faster. Let's make a run for it."

Angus nodded and kicked the starter. They were on their way.

TWO MILES FURTHER ON, they rounded a bend and saw what they thought were red flowers spread along a ditch, but up closer they saw it was blood and body remains. It was a hideous sight and Ray almost threw up. He saw Ginger shield her eyes, and Angus shake his head. The tigers had slaughtered an old woman, and she lay in bits and pieces. The tigers had barely fed on her.

Ray called out, "Remember to dump your packs if they're on us!"

They rode on for about three miles, then heard a huffing sound behind them. It was the tigers, breathing hard, closing on them from behind.

Ray yelled, "Cut your packs loose!" and pulled his belt knife to cut the line and dump his packs. The motorcycle immediately felt lighter and faster. Ray looked over to see Ginger fumbling with the line to drop the packs.

Angus called out, "I don't have my knife — I left it packed away!"

Ray rode in close to help cut their line, and just as he reached over with the knife, their top-heavy motorcycle hit a patch of clay, slid sideways, and lay on its side, sending Angus and Ginger rolling. The cats were on them with ferocious roars. Angus and Ginger both screamed, but not for long.

Ginger's last words were, "Oh, Angus."

They were dead within seconds, torn to pieces by the tigers. Ray cried in anguish as he turned his motorcycle to charge the tigers, riding right through them as they fed on his friends. The cats were busy and paid him little mind. One cat swatted at him as he went by, shredding his shirt and opening cuts on his cheek and arm. Their speed and strength terrified Ray. He turned the bike and rode through them again and was lucky to make it. He could see that Angus and Ginger were no more.

RAY CRIED WITH GREAT heart-rending sobs as he rode slowly along the road, which was now very rough. He felt a terrible guilt. Why hadn't he noticed that Angus had no belt knife to cut the load loose, as they planned? Angus had given Ray his own knife, saying he had another in his pack. Ray hadn't followed up to make sure. He'd been too busy looking at Ginger's ass, causing him to think about Giselle. He felt like scum.

Then Ray experienced a prolonged terror like he'd never known. He heard the huffing sound of the tigers again. They were coming for him, and the road was so rough he didn't think he could outrun them. The cats got to within twenty feet of him, but he was able to maintain just enough speed to stay ahead of them — just barely. The race went on for a mile. Ray could feel and smell the cats just behind him. Their odor was a blend of urine, blood, meat, and an earthy cat smell that made him want to throw up. Their huffing made him feel they were going to hit him from behind at any moment, no matter what he did. The race finally ended when the cats gave up or tired of their chase. Ray rode into the night.

Finally, curled up in four inches of water in a wooden culvert, Ray slept, hearing the huffing noise in his nightmares. When he woke up, he felt numb all over, and his hands shook. Maybe it was shock. When he remembered what happened, he started crying with his face in his hands. He sat in the culvert for an hour, oblivious to the water, and tried to block out the terrible memories.

Ray heard voices and saw a man and a woman looking at his motorcycle, jammed in the bushes. They wore coolie hats and rope sandals with tire treads for soles. Ray approached them, thinking, I must be a hideous sight. He was filthy and bleeding from cuts on his face and arm. They took no notice of his appearance but started signing and speaking in Chinese. The woman made claw marks with her hands, and the man signed stripes across his chest.

"Yes," Ray said, nodding. He could barely talk, his voice coarse from crying and yelling. The man made the claw mark sign and motioned down the road. The cats were gone. Ray waved goodbye and rode on, looking for a petrol station and directions. Ginger had been carrying the maps. He found a nearly hidden petrol station near a hut in the trees along side the road and topped off his tank. He asked directions, but the old man couldn't understand his questions, and looked at his disheveled appearance with sympathy. He said "Mao" and wouldn't take any money.

Chapter 13
Lotu and a Tough Crowd

Ray continued to ride and wondered why he wasn't hungry after all the hours on the road. Maybe he was dead already, like Angus and Ginger; a ghost, and riding this road was his hell. He rounded a bend and saw another ripped-up body by the road, blood everywhere. *"Ah Jesus. No. How much more of this can I take?"* he thought, as he slowed to see how fresh the kill was. Were the cats still near?

Then he heard a keening sound, whipped his head around to be sure he was safe, and spotted a little girl tucked between bamboo limbs in a thicket across a drainage ditch. Ray stopped, parked the bike and splashed toward her. Though she was filthy, she was a beautiful little girl, about five years old, with glittering black eyes. She was covered in sweat and had been crying. Ray approached her, not knowing what to say.

He said quietly, "Are you alright?"

To his astonishment, she gave a wistful small smile and said, "Yes, I think so."

Ray said, "You speak English?"

She looked at Ray with those eyes, capturing his heart. "Yes. I'm a Presbyterian," she said, nodding.

Ray remembered Gray's comment about the missionaries.

"My name is Lotu. The tigers got my uncle two days ago, after he put me here." She pointed to the body on the road, and started crying again. "I didn't know what to do. I was so scared."

Ray helped Lotu out of the bamboo. "Let's get out of here. Can you ride on the motorcycle with me?"

He picked her up and hugged her. She was warm and alive, not a ghost. He almost cried, holding her as he scrambled up the ditch.

"My name is Ray."

"U-lay?" Lotu said.

"No, Ray."

"Lay?"

Ray grinned. "Can't handle the r's up front, eh? How about Murphy?"

"Mu-phy," Lotu said with a nod, "Go to the liver, help is at the liver." She spoke, butchering the r's.

They rode about ten miles and came to a large river.

"Is that the Mekong River?" Ray wasn't sure where he was.

"Yes, my father calls it the 'Mighty Mekong.'"

The road led to a sheltered bay with a large war junk tied to a woven bamboo dock. As they approached the dock, Lotu twitched and said, "Ooo-wee, wrong junk. Thats Wu Song. Be careful, Mu-phy."

They were already close to the dock and were being watched by the crew. There was no turning back. The captain of the vessel stood on deck by a pilothouse that had a light machine gun mounted on a swivel. He was big for a Chinaman, with a gold braided coat, his hair in a "queue," the traditional Chinese ponytail, and a big Fu Manchu moustache. He looked formidable and mean. His crew was equally mean looking, and Ray saw several knives and guns. The captain held up his hand, indicating they should stop.

"Who might you be, at my dock?" Sitting on the boat deck, an old man wearing a Mongolian hat translated to English, looking at Ray's round eyes.

"I'm a traveler headed for the Spice Islands," Ray answered. He could feel Lotu making herself small behind him on the motorcycle. "We are just passing through."

"And the girl?"

Ray didn't like this interest in Lotu. "She's my traveling companion."

Wu Song bowed majestically, trying to look pleasant. "Looks like you've had trouble. Please, come aboard my ship to clean up and perhaps have some sport," he said through his translator.

Ray could see Wu Song eyeing his money belt, easily seen through his ragged shirt. They reluctantly boarded the junk; but were glad for a chance to clean up and get food. They walked past the Mongolian translator who was chained to the deck, with food and water in bowls at his feet, like food for a dog. A guard with a rifle stood nearby.

As they passed the Mongol, Ray asked, "Where'd you learn English?"

"I've got a cousin in Brooklyn," the translator answered. The guard grunted and indicated they should move ahead.

Ray and Lotu took spit baths from a bucket on the cargo hatch cover, and ate rice and fish from wooden bowls. Lotu repeated her warning, "Be very careful, Mu-phy."

Ray heard a chain being drug across the deck, and looked up to see Wu Song and the translator.

"We will have sport this afternoon on the fantail. It is American poker. I love the game. Do you play?"

Ray pondered the question, and seemed taken aback. "Well, I have played a little poker at the country club back home." It was Ray's standard answer. He'd never been in a country club in his life, and he was a shark at poker. It was at the core of his many fights.

Wu Song was pleased. He clapped his hands and gave a nod. "I will prepare the table," he said, leaving the translator standing there.

The Mongol looked at Ray and said quietly, looking at the floor, "Don't lose the girl. He will abuse her, sell her, eat her, or feed her to his dogs."

The guard nearby heard him talking and swatted the translator hard on the side of the head with his rifle butt, a terrible crunching sound. The Mongol lay on the deck, bleeding, probably dead. When Ray moved to check on him, the guard swung the gun around and motioned him away. Ray looked at Lotu. She nodded at him, showing no emotion. Ray thought, *"Man, this is a tough crowd."*

THE GAME BEGAN. THE stakes were Ray's money belt, the girl and the motorcycle, against a small sailing junk anchored in the bay. Lotu translated, saying that Wu promised the boat was in good shape, with a Buda engine.

Ray knew the game was a ploy to (honorably?) get his belongings and the girl in a sportsmanlike manner for — face? — ego? — he didn't know. What he did know was it would be ridiculous for Ray, from Odessa, Texas, to have a sailboat. Water was to put in your drink and run under bridges, for chrissake. But if he lost the game, he would have nothing and Lotu would be in trouble. If he won, he didn't think Wu Song would let them go.

As they began to play, Ray knew he could win. He'd picked up three "tells" from the big Chinaman almost immediately. *"This guy would be toast in the oilpatch,"* he thought.

Lotu translated, "The game is to be four out of seven. For everything."

"Like the world series," Ray thought. Ray played sloppily at first, to pick up the tells, then started bearing down to make the guy sweat, while he tried to figure out what to do. During the third game, Ray slowly pulled his belt knife out and put it on the table.

"Let's raise the stakes a little. How about this knife for the Mongol?"

"He's dead. What do you want him for?" Wu Song asked.

Ray smiled. "I saw his foot move. I may need a translator."

Wu Song laughed, "I'll make sure you will be together."

It was a chilling statement, and foretold Wu Song's plans.

Chapter 14
Trouble and Deliverance

Ray won the third, fourth and fifth game, and with the tally at three to two, he worried about the consequences of winning the next game. Would Wu Song be a gracious loser? Lotu sat quietly beside Ray, the guard watched from the door. Wu Song dealt the cards. The tension was palpable, with everyone engrossed in the game. They studied their hands.

Then a ratcheting sound was heard in the quiet air. Wu Song looked up and cut loose with a string of curse words. Another war junk had drifted in, to within fifty yards of their boat, unnoticed. The sound was the bolt being worked on an M-60 machine gun, mounted on the pilot house of the new vessel. The gunner was sighted in on the back deck, where they sat, and was tracking as the boat drew nearer. No one moved. Several other men on the new arrival's deck were holding guns sighted on Wu Song's crew, who stood frozen. It was obvious they were outnumbered and could be cut to pieces at any moment.

The new junk angled in slowly, with rope fenders out and spring lines ready, and tied up gunnel-to-gunnel with Wu Song's vessel. "River Dragon" was emblazoned in red on the length of the green hull of the new arrival. Various flags and pennants flew all over, and the ship bristled with guns.

A compact figure spoke from the deck, addressing the M-60 gunner, "Minoru, don't kill anybody yet, we must have a discussion first." The gunner nodded, but didn't relax.

The small, handsome man then said, "Permission to board," in English as he stepped onto Wu Song's junk without permission. He ignored Wu and turned toward Ray, "I am Chow Chee, captain of the Dragon. My apologies for interrupting your game. What are the stakes, Wu? I may want to play." Lotu translated for Wu.

As Wu Song told of the stakes in rapid Chinese, Ray scoped out the new arrival. He wore a coolie hat, and had a flowing black moustache, in contrast to a long red scarf. His vest-type flack jacket had a sewn-in holster on the left that housed a .45 automatic, butt forward, for a fast cross-draw. The .45 was cocked and locked, with the hammer back. Little birds and flowers were embroidered on his colorful jacket. Above the .45 hung two hand grenades of U.S. manufacture. Ray thought, as a river pirate, he looked scary but magnificent.

"Forgive me for interrupting. Please, go ahead and finish the game," Chow Chee said, and indicated they should continue.

"If I win this hand, I take the pot," said Ray, as he laid down a card. "I'll take one."

Wu Song grimaced as he took two cards. They showed their cards and Ray won the game, not knowing what to expect next.

"Congratulations! You've won the sailing junk and kept the girl," Chow Chee said, smiling at Ray. "Are you going to sell her?"

Ray reached out to collect his knife and said, "Not mine to sell. She's my traveling companion, joined me on that tiger-infested road."

Then a tall, thin man stepped in behind Chow Chee and said, "He's alive."

Chow snapped orders at him, "Get the chains off him. Take him to my bunk."

Wu looked at him incredulously. Everybody was standing now. The guard that had hit the Mongol was next to Wu, cleaning his fingernails with a knife. He was chewing khat, spitting over the rail, and staring arrogantly at Chow. His slung rifle still had blood on the stock.

Chow sighed. "Wu, you need to learn about honor and respect on my river."

Then he swiftly pulled the .45 and shot the guard in the face, blowing him backwards over the stern rail into the river, where he floated slowly downstream in a cloud of red. The spent cartridge from the .45 landed in the middle of the table. Blood and brain matter had spewed onto Wu's face and gold-braided coat, but he dared not move. Ray stood frozen in surprise.

Chow continued his statement in a normal tone of voice, as he reholstered the gun. "Don't be mistreating people, Wu — it's bad luck."

Then Lotu daintily reached over and picked up the spent cartridge, then stepped into Chow's arms and said sadly, "Father, the tigers got Uncle Mo."

Wu stood, beaten but transfixed. He'd had no idea who she was.

THE RIVER DRAGON PLOWED upstream, towing the sailing junk. Ray's motorcycle was lashed to the stern rail. Ray and Lotu cleaned up and slept the sleep of the dead, finally free of the numbing terror of the tigers. Not much was said for two days, while they recovered. The River Dragon was anchored in a sheltered loop of river, called an oxbow. It was quiet and peaceful, with goats grazing on a nearby bank.

Ray was told to meet the captain in the galley, which was surprisingly spacious and well-equipped. Ray looked for a spice rack, having eaten new and delicious foods aboard.

Chow Chee sat at the head of the crew's table. He had things to say. "Murphy, I want to thank you for saving my daughter. I am in your debt. You are welcome aboard the River Dragon for as long as you wish. What else can I do for you?"

Ray smiled, "Captain, you don't owe me anything. I don't keep a tally, favor-for-favor. I've only known Lotu for a few days, but I can tell you, I would do anything for her. You see, when I found her, I had given up; the tigers had taken everything from me. Saving Lotu gave me a reason to live again. Really, it's I that owe you, if we're keeping a tally."

Then Ray seemed embarrassed. "Sorry for the speech, captain. I've been drinking that disgusting arak with Altan, the Mongol."

Chow Chee laughed enormously, then regrouped. "Where are you headed, Murphy?"

"The Spice Islands. Indonesia."

Chow thought for a moment. "I may be able to help you."

TWO DAYS LATER, RAY was dozing in a hammock in the shade of the pilothouse, thinking about a new spice mix he'd found in the galley. The cook, Chang Ti, had said it was made with star anise, fennel seeds, a hot peppercorn and more, and it was used it in many Chinese dishes. Suddenly, a movement on shore froze his heart — the grass was rippling, over by the grazing goats. Something big was moving through the grass toward them. His stomach clutched. Was it the tigers?

"Jesus Christ!" he muttered as he saw an ear, "It's the tigers."

Without conscious thought, Ray scrambled up the companionway to the top of the pilothouse where the machine gun was mounted, covered with a canvas. As Ray ripped the cover off the gun, Minoru, the gunner, ran up, shouting, "No use — MY gun, my gun!"

Ray pointed toward the tigers, but it made no difference to Minoru, who waved him away as he shook his head and said, "No use, no use."

Desperate, Ray picked up Minoru and tossed him over the pilothouse rail into the river. Then he turned the gun, worked the bolt, and started firing a fifty-round belt toward the tigers. Inexperienced, he fired high. But quick to learn, he pulled the muzzle down and walked the rounds into the cats. They jumped and screamed, and swatted at the water, but Ray kept firing until the belt ran out. The tigers and two of the goats were dead, floating in a pool of blood by the shoreline.

When the gun stopped, Ray sagged against it, breathing hard. Then he noticed Minoru was having trouble in the water. Ray jumped over the rail to help him, but on the way down, realized, *"Fuck — I can hardly swim!"*

Ray and Minoru were both splashing helplessly in the water when Ray heard Chow say, "Now we got two in the water. Fish them out, and lock Min in the forecastle."

Ray thought, *"What?"* as they were pulled aboard.

Back on deck, Ray dried off while Minoru was hustled to the front of the boat.

Chow explained, "I have to lock him up to keep him from killing you, Ray. Your taking of the gun caused Minoru to lose face, and you also tossed him overboard. He will be coming for you. I may have to shoot him, and it's too bad. He's my best gunner."

"Jesus Christ," Ray said again, "Let's work this out. Don't shoot the guy."

Chow explained patiently, "Min is a goddamn Japanese. You don't turn them around. And I owe you for saving my daughter. So it pains me, but Minoru may have to die. He may do it by his own hand, like a samurai."

Ray shook his head, "Captain, by all that is holy, don't get hasty. We've got to find a way."

Ray went to the forecastle to speak with Minoru. Chow insisted that a guard go with him. "Hey, Minoru, sorry about the gun. I had to use it. Those tigers killed many people."

Minoru looked at him, showing no emotion. He was silent.

"Those tigers killed my friends, they killed Chow's brother, and almost got Lotu. So, I had to kill them, and now I'm asking your forgiveness for pushing you overboard. Please."

Minoru just sat there and looked at him. It was like talking to the wall. Ray gave up.

Later, Ray asked Chow, "Why can't you just fire him?"

Chow shook his head, "That won't work, Murphy. In matters of honor, he would go around the world to get you, to reclaim his honor."

Ray said, "Shit, what to do?" and went to drink some arak with Altan, who was getting better. The high point was when Lotu came by and kissed him for shooting the tigers that had killed Uncle Mo.

Ray was jumpy in the days ahead, worrying about Chow summarily carrying out the execution of Minoru. Ray sent money ashore with a crewman to pay for the goats he had accidentally killed.

EARLY ONE MORNING, Ray was helping the crew holystone the decks, when a lookout called, "Ahoy, the dugouts." Two dugouts were headed toward them, one smoking. The snapping clicks of safety's going off could be heard all over the junk; the smoking dugout could be a bomb. Shades of Wu Song.

The lead dugout was ringed with sticks of incense and had long, colorful streamers tied to the front. It was a Buddhist prayer boat. The coolie pushed the smoking dugout towards them, waved, and paddled away.

A canvas covered the contents of the dugout. They cautiously removed the canvas to reveal two tiger heads, and two scuffed, dusty backpacks. One was Ray's, and the bloody one belonged to Angus and Ginger. At the sight, Ray covered his face to hide his tears. He was embarrassed to cry in front of the stoic Chinese, but couldn't help it.

Chow Chee spoke, "Those Buddhist incense sticks are strong medicine. You have made High Honor, Murphy — for killing those mangy cats."

Then, they were blessed with what Ray felt was a miracle

When Minoru heard about the dugout ringed with incense sticks, he called Chow Chee to the forecastle, saying, "High Buddhist Honor for Mu-phy-san, I cannot kill him now. Also, I love Lotu, and Mu-phy saved her."

When Chow told Ray, he knew Lotu had made a case for Mu-phy.

Later, Ray lay in a hammock under the canopy of the fantail in a soft rain, and said, "Whew," in relief. "Life ain't a walk in the park on the Mekong."

RAY HUMMED TO HIMSELF as he carefully walked along the deck of the Dragon. He was barefoot like most of the crew, and had learned the folly of not avoiding the deck cleats, used for dock lines. Both of his feet were cut and bruised from earlier encounters with the cleats. He was headed for an after-breakfast session with Chang Ti, the boat's cook, who spoke better English than some roustabouts in the oilpatch. Chang explained his "English" was, like many in the area, due to missionary school, karaoke, and American movies. Honest-to-God, he sounded like Orson Welles.

Ray had been exploring the galley and wanted to know more about the Tianjin pepper, Chinese for "facing heaven." He'd heard of peppers referencing hell, but never heaven. Ray entered the galley, angling to keep his back to the wall. These days, when his back was to an open space, he had difficulty breathing and his hands shook. He hoped it was a brief aftershock of the terror from the cats closing in on him from behind, for what seemed like an hour on the motorcycle. Ray was wearing a coolie hat, pulled down over his hair, which seemed to be turning white. Due to the heat, he wore a Texas A&M t-shirt and Levi's, cut off just below the knees. A product of west Texas, he could not bring himself to wear "shorts."

"Good breakfast," Ray complimented the cook, always a safe bet, as he slid onto the bench of the galley table.

Chang Ti smiled, "You want to talk about the heavenly pepper, yes?"

"Yes, and the others, what are they?"

Chang answered, "We also use Sichuan peppers, Tien Tsin red peppers and a Red Sichaun peppercorn." Chang explained how the peppers were prepared and used.

Ray was wishing he could take notes, when he saw a picture on the bulkhead, of Chow Chee and a beautiful woman. As Chang finished his dissertation, Ray asked, "Lotu's mother?" pointing to the picture.

Chang looked down. "Yes, she was lost two years ago. Killed by the Qiantang River tidal bore, while visiting her sister in Yanguan. They were crabbing and didn't realize the time."

"A boar?" Ray asked. "Boars kill people, too?"

"No, it is a tidal bore. The Qiantang River has the largest tide in the world, a twenty-five-foot wall of water that rushes up the river twice a day. It's fast, and goes miles upriver, and takes out everything in its path."

Ray shook his head. "Holy shit! Rogue tigers, river pirates, monster tides — what's next?"

Chapter 15
Anything

Ray felt like he was back working in the oilfields of Odessa, as he crawled along the dirty diesel engine, checking belts, pulleys, fuel lines and oil levels. He was aboard his sailing junk, which he had won from Wu Song in the card game. Chow and Lotu were aboard visiting.

He asked Chow Chee, "Why would Wu bet a sailing junk against a motorcycle, a money belt and a little girl?"

Chow said, "Ah, Ray, he did it for sport. He was going to kill you anyway, then I showed up and ruined his plan."

Lotu was going through the pots and pans in the small galley, singing and pointing out what he needed. "You need a new wok, and a larger cooking pot, Mu-phy, to cook crab in. And if you're going to be a sailor, you need to learn your knots: bowline, reef knot, clove hitch, truckers hitch, you know."

Ray shook his head, "Where did you learn all of that? And why do you think I am going to be a sailor?"

"Well," Lotu said, "You **have** got a boat — learn your knots, dummy." and she giggled.

Chow laughed, "She's mothering you. Only five years old, yet she monitors my sweets and makes me eat vegetables." Chow grew serious. "But she's right. This is a good boat; you should learn to sail it. You can learn the basics in one afternoon, then spend the rest of your life learning the rest. It makes sailing interesting."

"Western boats are designed after fish that go through the water, whereas Chinese boats are designed after ducks that float atop the water," Chow went on. "Junks are easy boats to sail. You can go anywhere in southeast Asia in this boat, into the shallow rivers and bays, or even to the Spice Islands. Think about it."

It was quite a speech, and Ray could hardly get his head around it, so he asked the first thing that came to him. "Why do I need to learn knots?"

Chow explained, "Knots are much the same on all sailing vessels, to adjust sails and make the boat go. Also, my friend, with a boat you will learn a new language."

Ray looked at Lotu, who was nodding her head. "A new language?"

"Yes," Chow said, "more like the names of things on a boat. A wall is a bulkhead, the floor is the sole, except on top, when it's a deck. Left is port, and is red. Right is starboard, marked green. Rope is line when it's used, front is fore, back is aft. You see?"

"No, front is bow, back is stern!" sang Lotu, with a big grin.

Though some of the terms were familiar from his time on the M/V Irony, Ray shook his head in bewilderment. Lotu and Chow were laughing.

So, the sailing lessons began; the Spice Islands called. Ray liked his junk, with its large aft house for lounging, middle cabin with galley, head (toilet) and engine, and bunks forward for sleeping. The hull was teak, with leeboards for shallow water sailing. The many control lines running off of the fully battened sails on the two masts looked complicated, but were easy to operate. Ray mused that with a couple thousand years' experience, the Chinese had it right. He was astounded that the junk would sail into the wind, although at an angle.

Out of the oxbow, the Mekong River was wide, with slow current, perfect for sailing with a light breeze. Ray learned the basics quickly, became fascinated with sailing, and wanted to change the unfathomable Chinese name of his new boat to Water Dog, after a lizard he saw in a nearby creek.

Chow laughed and said, "You can do that, but not without a ceremony, paying tribute to Neptune, known to seamen as the mythical god of the sea. And for good measure, you should also make an offering to Mazu, the Chinese goddess of the sea." Already, Ray was learning about the superstitions of sailors.

Ray slept on the boat from their first days in the oxbow. His nightmares about the tigers caused him to scream in the night and the crew had driven him off the war junk. He was getting better, though, and had gained weight and let his beard grow out to cover up his scars. Now he looked less like a thug and more like an emaciated bear. Ray still could not have his back exposed to open spaces, without feeling like a tiger could hit him at any moment.

His hair was now completely white, and he covered it with a coolie hat that Lotu had given him. She had said, "You know, Mu-phy, with your white hair and sunglasses, you look like a movie star." He knew she was being kind. Behind his sunglasses, his eyes still showed the fears and losses that haunted him.

IN RAY'S NEW WORLD of boats, the pirate's long-tail fascinated him. It was a twenty-foot, narrow vessel that functioned as the "ships boat," used to take crew to shore and make provisioning runs. The long-tail had a small automobile engine literally balanced on its transom with a long shaft (tail) protruding to a propeller in the water. The other end of the shaft became the tiller, used to articulate the engine to steer. It was pure Thailand in design and Ray wanted a ride in it.

Chang Ti, the cook, who had become his friend, laughed and said, "Not this time, Ray, we will be loaded to the gills on the way back. Next time, we'll make room for you."

Ray was delighted. He wanted to see how this strange machine worked. Chang Ti and two crew headed downstream to the village market for supplies.

The next morning, Ray lay in his bunk on Water Dog (they'd done the ceremony), looking at his feet and wondering if they were still growing. He'd slept well for the first time, no dreams of Giselle or the tigers.

"Mu-phy, come quick," Lotu called out from the war junk. Water Dog was rafted alongside.

Ray slid open the hatch. "What?"

"Chang Ti did not return last night. He's coming up the oxbow now, very slowly."

They could hear the engine on the long-tail misfiring, as it slowly approached. The boat was awash, water up to the seats. It was shot to pieces. The two crew lay face down, draped over bundles of provisions, water sloshing with the movement of the long-tail. Chang Ti sat with one arm useless, and the other draped over the tiller, steering by moving his body. Chang was clear-eyed, but bleeding out his mouth, blowing bubbles, from a lung shot.

He looked up at Chow Chee, nodding his head, "It's Wu Song . . . he has help now. Two more war junks . . . from downriver. They just opened up on us, Chow, they . . . "

They all stood by the rail, waiting for Chang to continue, but he was dead. Lotu started crying. Ray turned and went back to his boat, and leaned over his stern rail, looking into the water, trying to calm himself. Then the water turned pink. It was Chang Ti's blood, washing by in the current. Ray lost it and started crying. It was too many losses, too much. As he cried, he kept saying "goddamn, goddamn, goddamn." His hands shook.

AN HOUR LATER, RAY had recovered a bit. He washed his face, thought of RD Carrera for some reason, then went to find Chow Chee. He found Chow with his remaining crew at the large galley table, in a war council. Ray didn't ask permission to join, he just moved in and sat down.

When Chow looked at him sympathetically, Ray said, "What can I do?"

Chow gave a sad smile, "We were just wondering what you can do for us."

Ray looked him in the eyes and said, "Anything."

Chow considered this statement. "Anything?"

Ray looked at him steadily. "Yes. Anything."

Chow was taken aback. He'd seen Ray crying over the rail an hour ago, and had written him out of his bold plan. The Yankee had recovered quickly.

Chow laid out his plan, suddenly enhanced by Ray's participation. "We know Wu Song's habit of rafting their junks together at night, for security, to prevent boarding parties. This can work to our advantage. It appears we are outgunned by about three to one, so we need diversion and surprise. We will float a fire-ship down on them with the current. Minoru is bringing an old sampan with more crew as we speak. We will fire it, loaded with explosives, and follow up with an attack." Chow grinned, like he was enjoying this, and added, "As we attack and Wu Song is distracted, the Water Dog will sail down the far side of the Mekong, past the firefight, unnoticed."

Ray looked at Chow in stunned silence, "No. I won't run. I know I said I'd do anything, but why do you want me to sneak away?"

Chow laughed. "Minoru and Altan the Mongol will go with you — and Lotu. I don't want her in this war. I want you to take her to the city of Kuah on the island of Langkawi in Malaysia. My cousin, Maximillian Chee is there."

Ray interrupted, "But don't you need us all here? We're outgunned!"

Chow nodded. "What I need of you, Ray, is more important than another gun in a firefight. I need to know that Lotu is safe. I need you to keep her safe, and enroll her in the Presbyterian school in Kuah under an assumed name. Max will help you."

Ray was looking at Chow, sort of wide eyed.

Chow explained further, "Besides being good with a gun, Minoru is a good sailor, and can navigate to Kuah, no problem. Altan can translate for you, and he needs a doctor for his head wound."

After some thought, Ray raised his hand. "One question, captain. Will Min remember that he changed his mind about killing me?" Everybody laughed.

Chow said, "You will do okay, Mu-phy. I'm not worried about you."

THE CREW ON THE RIVER Dragon prepared for war. Guns were cleaned and ammunition stashes were inventoried. When a scout was sent downriver for reconnaissance, Ray donated his motorcycle to the cause. The sampan was loaded with explosives and made ready as a fireship. They waited for a moonless night for the attack.

Chow called Ray to his quarters and gave him an envelope. "Here is a letter of introduction to my cousin. Max has done well, owns a hotel and restaurant in Kuah, and is building another. Explain the situation to Max and he will help you. I've asked him to employ you for a while, so you can make sure Lotu settles in okay, Max has never met her. Minoru will come back upriver. I need him." Chow frowned. "Ray, am I asking too much? I know you're headed for the Spice Islands."

Ray laughed, "Chow, you don't need to ask. Lotu is very special to me. Can't you tell I'm having a good time?"

Chow smiled, "I knew you would say that. Here's something else." He handed Ray a vest-type flak jacket with a .45, like his. "Take this with you, it's my old one. Also, one other thing." He draped a moonstone necklace on a leather thong over Ray's head. "For good luck, please wear it at all times. And if you really need better luck, there are two diamonds behind the stone, take them to Singapore to cash in."

The reconnaissance scout returned with good news. The three war junks were rafted together downriver like big fat targets. Chow's crew cheered. The loss of their friends made this war personal. Chang Ti had been very popular. Chow Chee was everywhere, giving orders. Their meticulous preparations astounded Ray. On Water Dog, he was told, "No lights anywhere, and rags wrapped on the oarlocks. Sound travels on water." and "Poles and oars to fend off the bank if drifting too close." Fuel topped off, navigation charts ready.

Once past Wu Song, Water Dog's route would be down to the Mekong Delta, across the Gulf of Thailand, past Singapore, then up the Malacca Strait, dodging pirates in the mangroves, to the island of Langkawi, in Malaysia. A long trip, so the junk was well supplied.

"More pirates?" Ray had asked. He thought they were the main pirates around.

Chow laughed, "Ray, my friend, pirates are everywhere. Have you talked to your banker lately?"

Lotu came on board Water Dog with an unbelievable amount of luggage, and said she was almost six and would need more school clothes. Chow just shook his head. Ray had argued that he and Minoru stay and help with the fight, especially since Minoru was his best gunner. Chow would have none of it.

"Lotu means the world to me, and I cannot risk losing her. You and Min are her best chance out of here, and for that, I am again indebted to you."

"Ah, you owe me nothing," Ray said

Chapter 16
Sharks, a Bar, and a Party

The fireship was spectacular. As planned, it drifted with the current, down on Wu's wooden junks in complete darkness. When finally spotted, with a fuse sputtering on deck, gunfire from Wu's crew did nothing to slow it down. It was blazing as it crashed into the rafted junks with sparks flying, and then exploded. The River Dragon followed behind, with guns blazing, raking the decks of Wu's junks. Chow Chee could be heard yelling orders, and his crew was screaming in revenge, as they fired round after round into the killers of their friends.

Far across the wide Mekong, Water Dog steered quietly along the bank. Minoru was at the tiller, peering into the darkness. Ray was at the starboard rail, pole ready to fend off the bank if they drifted too close. Altan, still not feeling well, was in a hammock. Lotu was on the foredeck, giving quiet commentary on the battle.

"I can see in the flashes, Daddy steering across their transoms for stern shots."

Ray shook his head, "Goddamn, Lotu, five years old and you sound like a pirate already."

Lotu giggled. "I'm almost six!"

It looked as if the surprise had worked, the battle was going well, and the ship and crew aboard Water Dog were on their way to Malaysia, then the Spice Islands.

THE NEXT MORNING, RAY was off the tiller and Minoru was steering again. It was a beautiful day, with a gentle breeze blowing them downriver. The junk was sailing effortlessly, all sails out, doing five knots. Altan was still in his hammock and Lotu was in the galley preparing lunch.

Ray thought, *"Such a pretty day, what could go wrong?"* He was kicked back, with his feet up in the seat, writing another letter to Giselle, telling of his adventure. He'd been posting the letters to Paris, even in the backwaters of China. Today he remembered Giselle's comment on his "special skill," and it caused him to smile. Their routine in Odessa had been to meet at the diner, explore different spices for a while, then go to the camper and fuck like mink. Afterwards, they would lay in bed and Giselle would teach him French, including her fifty favorite French curse words.

Once, finishing such a session, Giselle lay back and said, "Ray, I have to say, you do have a special talent."

Ray had blushed, and said, "Why, thank you, Giselle."

"Not that!" she had answered, laughing, "I mean with languages. You pick up languages very quickly."

Ray was beginning to realize he could understand some of the Chinese spoken around him. At least, maybe, he had <u>that</u> skill.

ONE DAY, RAY WAS WEARING the flak jacket and pistol, to get used to the weight. The pistol was loaded, and he practiced working the slide. Being a Texan, he was embarrassed that the most lethal weapon he'd used in Odessa was a pool cue. He would have to learn. As Ray basked in the sun, writing his letters, he heard Minoru mutter about the steering.

Ray checked the stern of the boat, "Min, it looks like the lashings attaching the rudder are coming loose."

"No problem," Min said, "I will re-lace the lashings."

They struck the sails, and Minoru went over the side with fresh lashing in his mouth to make the repair, with the crew looking on. Ray was fascinated by the intricate figure eight weave Minoru used, which functioned as a perfect hinge. Lotu, of course, was giving advice, and Altan was standing by the rail. Suddenly, there was an explosive splash by Min, and he screamed. Something was attached to his thigh, jerking viciously, writhing in the water.

They saw a dorsal fin and Altan yelled, "Bull shark!"

As Ray pulled the .45 and thumbed the safety, he asked, "Sharks in the river?"

"Freshwater sharks in all the rivers," Altan said, as Ray started firing.

"Seven rounds and I can't hit the damn thing — it's moving too much!"

Lotu yelled, "I think you hit Min!"

Minoru was floating in a pool of blood, drifting away from the boat, stunned but moving. The shark was biting at his own back, but moving away from Min.

"I must have hit the shark," Ray said as he grabbed a line, tied it to his waist, handed one end to Altan, and jumped over the stern, hearing Lotu's words, "You can't swim!"

Ray hit the water, splashing, trying to get to Minoru, but the weight of the flak jacket pulled him down.

"Shit, forgot about it," Ray thought as he sank, trying to get it off. He could hear Lotu shouting. He was about out of air, still struggling with the straps when he felt something grab his hair and pull up, and he broke the surface. Min had grabbed him as he floated by. They hit the end of the line, and Altan and Lotu pulled them in. Face to face as they were pulled in, Min held his other hand to what was left of his earlobe.

Bleeding profusely, Minoru said, "You shot me!" and laughed hysterically. "But you got the shark, too!"

Ray started laughing too, and they kept laughing as they rolled around in the blood on the back deck.

Then Minoru grabbed Ray and said, "Ray-san, tell me, who saved who?" and laughed some more, ecstatic to be free from the freshwater bull shark.

To everyone's amazement, Minoru's shark bite amounted to several deep puncture wounds and bad bruises. They'd expected a bloody stump. The wounds were doctored and dressed, and Min retired to his bunk to dream about his latest adventure. Ray had sewn up what was left of Minoru's ear, telling him he had experience, from sewing up an ear on M/V Irony.

Ray leaned over the transom and checked the rudder lashings. Min hadn't quite finished before he was attacked by the shark.

"Somebody needs to finish lashing the rudder," he said.

Lotu gave it a quick glance. "Mu-phy. You go," she suggested.

Ray shook his head, peering at the water, expecting a shark at any moment. "I ain't getting in that water. You're agile and quick, just ease down there quietly and do it. I'll cover you with the pistol."

Lotu laughed, "In your dreams. You'll shoot me, like you did Min."

Altan spoke up from the hammock, heading them off, "I'd do it, but my coordination's bad, with this concussion and all."

Lotu looked at him, "I don't know, Altan. Your coordination seems pretty good these days, when you're reaching for my biscuits."

It was a stalemate. No one was brave enough to go into the water. In the end, they butted Water Dog up to the bank, and nervously, Ray lashed the rudder, while standing in the mud, collecting leeches on his bare legs.

RUDDER REPAIRED, THE sail down the Mekong toward the delta was uneventful. Min's bite wounds were treated by a tried-and-true Chinese potion, but they worried about fever, a sign of infection. Minoru was more talkative, glad to be alive, and sat nearby the helm to continue the sailing lessons.

"You may become a good sailor someday, Ray-san, if you live long enough."

Ray wasn't sure what that meant; would he live long but learn slowly, or would his learning be cut short by an early demise? At this point, Ray figured it was a coin toss.

The wind generally blew downriver in the morning hours, and upriver in the afternoon. So, morning sailing was with the wind, sails out, easy going. Into the wind in the afternoons required them to tack back and forth across the broad Mekong to make headway. It was good experience for Ray, but mentally exhausting and physically active, as he was doing most of the work himself.

On the third day after the shark attack, they celebrated Lotu's sixth birthday.

"Six years old, going on thirty," Ray said.

Minoru, Ray and Altan banished Lotu topside to steer (after all, she was now six), so they could bake a cake. Min wanted to make Japanese rice cakes, Altan insisted it must have horse's milk, a Mongolian favorite. Ray wanted an American birthday cake. The final result was a disaster, but edible. They decorated it with six beans in a smiley face on top. Lotu beamed when she saw it, but suddenly looked sad.

"I wish daddy was here."

Not thirty, just six.

ALTAN WAS AT THE HELM when they approached the mouth of the Mekong, emptying into the Gulf of Thailand. Minoru and Lotu started securing everything, including themselves, with tethers.

Ray was startled, "What's going on?"

Altan explained, "We will be crossing the bar soon, and it can be dangerous."

Ray nodded, "Been my experience, all bars are dangerous."

"River bar, my friend," Altan laughed, "Much more dangerous than a drinking bar. You should hook up with a tether or safety line. We have to cross it just right, at slack or flood tide, or you can lose your boat or maybe your life."

Ray felt ignorant. He'd paid no attention to the river bar crossings on M/V Irony.

"How do you know when?"

"Ya gotta know the tides, brother. The Mekong tide range is almost four meters, so you have to pay attention."

"Yeah, Chang Ti told me about the tide that took Lotu's mother."

Ray helped tie everything down on the boat and wished he had a drink. They crossed the bar at high slack tide and made it fine. Ray promised himself to learn more about tides.

The plan was to cross the Gulf of Thailand, round the Malay peninsula to Singapore, to get a doctor to look at Altan, who still wasn't right after the concussion. After Singapore, they'd head up the Malacca Strait to the island of Langkawi, Malaysia. The passage to Singapore was about seven days if the weather was good. Ray flirted with seasickness the first day offshore, but soon got better. On the fourth day, Ray was steering on a nice beam reach, with good boat speed, enjoying the ride. He unhooked his safety line and took off his shirt, enjoying the sun.

Altan shook his head, "You need to hook up again. With these whitecaps, if you fell off the boat, it's a death sentence. We would turn around, but would never find you in the waves. And don't forget, some drowned sailors are found unzipped, — they fall off while taking a leak."

Feeling humbled, Ray hooked up his tether and got back on the tiller.

Lotu came on deck, looking serious. Ray knew the look.

"What?" he said.

"We may have two for the doctor in Singapore. Min's got a fever."

THE SEA GOD NEPTUNE and goddess Mazu blessed them with a fine trip. As they approached Singapore, they hid the guns and put up the yellow quarantine flag, getting ready for boarding by customs and immigration. They cleared in, with relief. Min's slight fever could have kept them out. They tied up at a dock in a bay on Sentosa Island and discovered their "sea legs," walking and weaving down the dock. The island's development office referred them to a doctor willing to look at both Minoru and Altan, and helped them schedule an appointment for the afternoon. The crew had time for a meal in a nice restaurant, then trouped into the doctor's office. The doctor was East Indian, and asked if either Minoru or Altan had objections to a Hindu doctor.

Minoru answered, "Doctor, we have been neck deep with heathens, Muslims, Hindus, Buddhists, and even Christians. Why should I worry about one more Hindu?"

The doctor hemmed and hawed, looking into Altan's eyes, gave coordination tests, and said he would be okay in time, with light duty. Altan smiled. Then Minoru's leg wounds were checked and re-bandaged, and he was given antibiotics. The doctor frowned while looking at the repair job on Min's ear, but said nothing.

The doctor said, "If you have nothing against the Hindu, I suggest you attend the Deepavali Festival going on now in Singapore's India town. It is a celebration of good over evil, or light over darkness. And looking at your friends, I think you would enjoy its excellent beer garden."

The crew of the Water Dog, waiting in the foyer, heard this. Ray was first to respond.

"Great idea, doctor, right after we go to Raffles for our Singapore Slings."

Lotu looked at the doctor seriously, and said, "We know about evil."

The Raffles Hotel, famous as the originator of the Singapore Sling, the gin and juice drink that put it on the map in 1915, was just down the road. The crew made their way past the seven-foot turbaned Indian doormen, went straight to the bar and ordered the drinks. Lotu was denied entrance, but could be seen sitting in the lobby tapping her foot.

With Singapore Slings all around, they raised a toast. "Here's to Chow Chee and the crew of the River Dragon!" Ray said, loud enough for Lotu to hear. She raised her hand in salute. The drinks were delicious.

"Min, are you sure you should be drinking, taking those meds?" Altan asked.

Min smiled, "You're on meds too, so you don't get my drink, you barbaric Mongol!" and they all laughed.

Ray nodded at the painting of the full-length nude behind the bar. "My friend Clink Parker from M/V Irony told me about her. Didn't think I'd see her so soon. I wonder where Clink is today?" He thought about the friends he had met and left, and those he had lost on his journey.

After finishing their drinks, they thought about food, and the beer garden in India town. And Lotu was waiting. Maybe they could sneak her into the garden. Feeling extravagant, they caught a cab to the Deepavali Festival.

The celebration was just what the crew needed, after the stresses of the river war, the river itself, and the open ocean crossing. In the streets of India town, they listened to the music and watched the dancers and banners flying — and began to celebrate and relax. They ate, drank toasts to everything they could think of, and sang along with the music. The beer, in tubs of tall unmarked bottles labeled "Strong" and "Stronger," was good, and they sampled both, emptying a number of bottles. Lotu was daintily taking sips of the stronger brown beer. None of them were feeling any pain.

A warm rain started and many in the crowd sought shelter, but the Water Dog crew and other hardy partiers sat in the rain and drank, enjoying the sights and each other. As the party ramped up, Lotu decided to dance on the table to the song "Dancing Queen" as she sang along.

Ray was impressed, "Hey Lotu, I didn't know you were a fan of Abba."

Between gyrations, Lotu said, "We have radios in China, Mu-phy. Did you think we were uncivilized?"

Ray laughed. "Abba ain't that civilized."

Then Altan threw up on an empty chair by a Chinaman, who made a comment about Mongols.

Altan was incensed. "Well, you had to build a ten-thousand-mile wall to keep us from coming down here and kicking your ass!"

The fight started and Ray scooped Lotu off the table, amid flying beer bottles. Ray looked to Minoru for help, but he was asleep, sitting up in his chair in the rain. Authorities came, broke up the fight, and asked the Water Dog crew to leave. On the cab ride back to the boat, all agreed that they had a wonderful time.

Chapter 17

Maxmillian, Not the Last Knight

Rested and refreshed from the good times at the Deepavali Festival, the crew of the Water Dog prepared the vessel for the trip up the Malacca Strait. The Sentosa development manager, whom they'd befriended with two bottles of the strong brown Indian beer, stood at the dock giving advice. Dahl was East Indian, complete with a turban, and spoke with a melodious high-pitched lilt.

"You have food, fuel and water, I see; do you have weapons, only for defense, of course?"

Ray looked at Dahl, wondering if he was also a cop. "Why would we need weapons?" he asked innocently.

"Ah, yes. You see, there may be pirates in fishing boats or small boats hiding in the mangroves along the edges of the Malacca Strait. They're rumored to be Indonesian Navy guys, moonlighting on second jobs at night."

Minoru shook his head, with a little smile, "Pirates seem to be everywhere."

"Ah, yes," Dahl said, "They can also come down the Johor Strait. You know about the strait that separates Singapore from Malaysia? During the big war, the Japanese came down the Malay peninsula on bicycles, rafted across the Johor, and surprised the

English, who had their guns set up for an assault from the sea. The guns were facing the wrong way! You saw the forts on the other side of this island. That's where the English lost Singapore forever — it is history, you see."

Minoru, the Japanese, looked at Dahl. "Yes. I lost two uncles, coming down the Malay peninsula." he said, "It's a small world."

"What happened to that boat?" Ray asked, pointing to a nearby boat that looked abandoned.

"Ah, yes," Dahl said, looking sad. "That is a mystery. This young happy couple sailed in, tied up to the dock and went to town for lunch, and vanished. The police conducted a search, but are puzzled. No trace of them was ever found."

Ray looked at Lotu. "We should stay alert, there is evil out there."

"Sometimes you sound like my daddy," Lotu sniffed.

The Water Dog departed Singapore, heading into a massive "traffic jam" of freighters, fishermen, tugs, barges, workboats and floating cranes in this small but bustling seaport. They had to avoid several new islands of dredgings, and spoils being built to expand Singapore. Finally, they left the busy city and crossed the Johor Strait, heading up the Malay peninsula toward the island of Penang. They watched the mangroves for pirates, and were surprised by several fishing boats racing towards them, only to pass just feet in front of their bow before racing off again. It was nerve wracking, wondering if they were to be hit, or boarded, or what. Minoru said that the fishermen were trying to throw off their "bad luck" by passing so closely.

Soon they were fighting headwinds and adverse currents, and finally had to use the diesel engine. At a fuel stop in the island city of Penang, they noticed another abandoned boat, and were told a similar story — its occupants had vanished.

"That's a fine boat; you wouldn't just leave it. So was the one we saw in Singapore. What the hell is going on?" Ray said.

Altan, somewhat of a cynic, said, "Maybe they couldn't make their boat payments."

WITH THE BOAT RUNNING well, Ray went below and sat in the saloon, thinking about what he'd learned about Max from Chow Chee. He looked at Chow's letter of introduction that he was to give to Max upon arrival in Langkawi. Ray wanted to be ready. Chow had said Max was named after Maxmillian, said to be the last knight in the middle ages. Max's father was persecuted in China for his religion, having to live on dog's milk as a child, as food was sparse. On migrating to Malaysia, his goal was to never go hungry again, and he became a successful businessman, to Max's benefit, who had inherited a hotel and restaurant, plus other properties and companies. Max spoke five languages and was constantly expanding his operations.

Ray thought, *"Who better to give me a job, so I can look out for Lotu's interests for a while?"* As he prepared to go topside again, he thought, *"Maxmillian Chee must be a giant of a man to accomplish all of that."* He was to be surprised.

The voyage to Langkawi was delayed three days by high winds and heavy seas. Water Dog found shelter in a small bay, where they rolled in the backwash, ate most of their food, and drank all the booze. They played poker during the wait and Ray cleaned everybody out, gave the winnings back, then won it back again. At this point, his popularity took a dip, and they quit playing poker for a while.

Finally, they nosed the junk into a mangrove-infested anchorage just outside the city of Kuah, on the island of Langkawi, home of Max Chee. Other boats were scattered in the mangroves and at first, they thought of pirates. But the mangroves grew out into the water and offered excellent protection from wind and waves. The boats belonged to locals and ex-pats who called the anchorage Hole-in-the-Wall, as it practically hid the anchored boats. With a stream of advice from everybody, Ray anchored the junk and secured it to mangroves to keep it from swinging, and soon they were ready to go to town.

"I'm hungry and tired of boat food," Lotu proclaimed.

Ray smiled, "This is a good opportunity to meet Max. He owns a restaurant, right?"

Walking on an unmoving dock with their sea legs made them chuckle as they tried to walk straight. At the top of the rickety dock, they found a phone line for a taxi, and they made the call. They had all cleaned up but still looked like a motley crew. Minoru's leg was bandaged, with a little blood here and there on his cut-open pant leg. Altan, the Mongol, looked as he always did, like a Mongol. Ray was bushy-faced and sunburned, with his jeans cut off below the knees. Lotu looked like a sassy wayward orphan. They negotiated Chinese yuan for Malay ringgit with the taxi driver, checked in with customs and immigration officials, and were soon on their way to meet Max.

As the taxi pulled up to the portico of the Atlas Hotel, Ray asked the question, "Hotel desk to find Max, or the hotel restaurant?"

"Food!" came the chorus from the crew. "We want food!"

"Let's order everything on the menu," Altan said, and they all laughed.

While waiting for their meals, they experienced the surreal feeling brought on by the quick change from a pitching boat, worrying about pirates, to the civilized surroundings of the restaurant. So much change, so quickly. The table and chairs seemed to move, more of the "sea legs" effect.

A small, bespectacled man approached, with a regal air. "Welcome to Langkawi," he said, "Breakfast is on me, and your rooms are being prepared, of course." He gave a big smile, "You must be Lotu. I loved your mother, and you look a lot like her. She was one of my favorites. I've been looking forward to your arrival."

At last, they had made contact with Maxmillian Chee. He was not what Ray expected. Ray was stunned — Max looked like a small, Chinese version of Rolando D. Carrera. They had the same black horn-rimmed glasses, widows peak, hair combed straight back. Ray was speechless.

As Lotu chatted and introduced everyone, Ray thought, *"Why does he remind me of Carrera, when he is half RD's size, and a Chinaman? Must be the glasses. No — it's his mannerisms, the way he looks straight at you and listens intently to what you had to say. Was that it?"* He didn't know, but he knew immediately that he liked Max, and they would probably have adventures together. They were kindred spirits, he could tell, without reservation.

MAX PEERED DOWN AT the letter of introduction. He and Ray were in his office, drinking Presidente beer. "Chow wants you to look after Lotu as she settles in at the Presbyterian boarding school. And you need a job as you do this?"

"Yes," Ray said. "I promised Chow, and he wasn't sure of your situation."

"I could easily take care of Lotu, Ray, but I understand about promises. And she seems very fond of you. You were a ship's cook and crane operator?"

"Yes, I shifted back and forth, as needed."

"Could you do that for me? I'm building a hotel, and I can use a cook."

Ray smiled, "Crane operator or cook's wages?"

Max laughed. "You're hired."

RAY WAS BACK ON A GRILL, cooking "western food" for tourists. It felt like deja vu all over again, except he was over ten thousand miles from Odessa, and he was the only non-Asian employee. But he had settled in easily and already he was ordering more spices for his grill. He could hardly believe the Spice Islands were not far away.

"Hey, how about some service, here!"

He looked up to see Lotu beaming across the counter. She looked rested and refreshed, and was wearing a new school uniform.

"The Presbyterians put you in a uniform, I see. Do they know how unruly you can be?"

Lotu made a face, "They don't even know my real name. I can be as ugly as I want." She laughed. "The food is not very good there, and they don't let me talk, but I like my roommate."

Ray spent his evenings writing letters; to Giselle, catching up on his adventures since his last letter, to Miss Teel and RD back in Odessa, and to Clink, care of the M/V Irony in Hong Kong. He sent them off, not knowing when or if they would be read, but it felt good to settle his feelings by writing.

Minoru and Altan had headed back to River Dragon on the Mekong after a few days' rest, with promises to let Ray and Lotu know how things were going upriver. Wu Song was a menace, and they worried what he might do if he had survived Chow's attack. Ray was at the grill for a few weeks before Max came by with a question.

"Ray, how good are you with a crane? And please tell it like it is, because this is a dangerous crane job with a high building, a long reach and heavy loads. You could get killed, or could kill somebody else." He paused. "So really, how good are you?"

Ray laid down his spatula, looked Max in the eye, and said, "Max, not to brag, but I'm probably the best crane operator you'll ever see."

And he was, both efficient and quick with the difficult jobs, saving Max time and money. Not bad for a short order cook. Soon Ray was earning full crane operator's wages, even when cooking.

MAX ASKED RAY TO STOP by his office. "You've been a big help here, and I'd be glad to give you a job for as long as you'd like. But Chow's letter of introduction says you're going to the Spice Islands. Do you mind telling me why? I have an interest in spices for business reasons. There's a huge mark-up in spices."

Ray briefly told his story, about Giselle and his quest.

"Do you know the distance and route? It's over two thousand miles, down the Malacca Strait and Java Sea."

"Yeah, I got the charts," Ray said, "I'm saving up for a crew, I can't do it myself."

They were drinking Presidente again, and Ray took a sip. "When Lotu is comfortable in school, and I'm satisfied she's safe, I'll look for crew." He paused and thought before continuing, "I think Wu Song had a bead on Lotu, she's such a beautiful girl. With him out there somewhere, I worry about her. Also, my junk needs work before the trip."

Max smiled. "The Phuket boatyard, just north in Thailand, can get your boat ready."

Ray nodded. "You sound interested in the trip, Max, do you want to go?"

Max laughed, "You see right through me. Let's make sure Lotu is settling in, then talk about it. She's my niece, you know."

As Ray experimented with spices, Max became more interested. Ever the entrepreneur, Max said, "You know, the Dutch have had a corner on spices for three hundred years. They controlled the Spice Islands, made huge profits. We can start a spice company, Ray, if we can get a supplier, and head the Dutch off at the pass."

Ray gave a sad smile. "I just want to walk Ambon and look at the spices growing, like Giselle and I dreamed. After that, we can do whatever you want."

Max invited Ray to visit the food stalls around Langkawi with him, to sample the exotic foods and spices of the Orient. They rode 125cc scooters, small and maneuverable, to explore even the smallest "kitchens" in alleys and byways, trying wide varieties of tasty, and sometimes unrecognizable, morsels. Max would describe the origins of the dishes, the special spices or techniques used in preparation. Ray realized Max was what was to become commonly known as a "foodie," one who enjoyed the pursuit of good cuisine in any form. Max would be waiting when Ray got off work. They would hop on the scooters and buzz through the busy intersections, dodging traffic, yelling directions to the next food stall over the noise. To Ray, it was fry-cook heaven.

After a busy week for both of them, Max stopped by the grill. "Hey Ray, I'm taking the train to Phuket on a quick business trip. Want to come along? We can check out the Thai food stalls and take a look at the boatyard for Water Dog."

"Good idea," Ray said, "The Dog needs the bottom cleaned and painted, and rigging checked. If Lotu's behaving at school, I'm up for the trip."

Ray enjoyed the train ride to Thailand, and was amazed at the change at the Thai border, from mosques every thousand yards, to statues of Buddha — from Muslim to Buddhist — by crossing an imaginary dotted line between countries. The first thing Ray noticed about Phuket was the many wide-open bars and "come-hither" women.

Max explained, "Muslims don't drink alcohol, so they limit the number of bars in Malaysia. And in Malaysia, if you get too friendly with a Muslim woman, elders will come around and have a very stern talk with you. Now, in Thailand, the Buddhists have a different agenda, we'll say, and companionship, alcohol, whatever, can be purchased, no problem. But be careful, some of the Thai women are "lady-boys," and they can be exceptionally beautiful. It's a very different culture."

Ray, who loved women, smiled and said, "Very interesting. I'll count my bahts, and check under their skirts early on."

The food court in Phuket was wonderful. They sampled almost every stall.

"Hey Max, have you tried the nasi goreng?"

"Ray, check out the spring rolls, and how about that pad thai?"

"These deep fried shrimp are great, but why are they so crunchy? ...What? We're eating the heads and shells and legs???"

Laughing and joking, and about to burst from gluttony, Max and Ray ventured over to Phuket's boat yard.

Max explained the yard's appeal, "You see the many tram-like rails, for pulling any type of boat into the yard for work. There are boats of all kinds; sloops, schooners, fishing boats, ships — and look, there in the corner is a war junk. You can see the gun ports."

As they looked at the big junk, Max felt Ray stiffen and grow quiet. He looked at Ray.

"What's wrong?"

"Nothing," Ray said, "When is your business meeting?"

"Later this afternoon, then we're scheduled to catch the train at 5:00 pm, just about happy hour," he laughed.

Ray did not laugh, he was quiet.

"You okay?" Max asked.

Ray said, "Max, I'm going to stick around Phuket for a few days, okay? Can you take care of Lotu?"

Max grinned, "The women, eh?"

Ray didn't answer.

Chapter 18
Wu Song, and Chow Chee's Reach

Wu Song had looked forward to bringing his war junk to Phuket for repairs. He'd been lucky. The fireship and Chow Chee's gunners had destroyed the two other junks, but he had escaped with a shot-up boat, losing half of his crew. His planned revenge for Chow Chee would be exquisite, and involve Lotu, his major fixation. From the first day he'd seen Lotu, on the riverbank with the Yankee, he'd fantasized about what he'd do to her. She was beautiful and had so much spirit, he looked forward to breaking her down. Time was against him though, she was getting older, and Wu liked them very young.

Phuket appealed to Wu because of its wide-open ways, no threat to his tastes. This time, Wu had contacted a procurer to arrange his "dates." Wu smiled as he laid out the polaroids of his past victims, to view and remember with excitement. The crew never entered his aft cabin, thinking Wu wanted privacy to pray. The crew never saw the special chute at the transom, where Wu would bleed his finished "toy" and drop it overboard for the sharks. But now that his boat was hauled out for repairs, he'd made other arrangements.

Wu thought of tomorrow with anticipation. The procurer ran an opium den, and had promised a day of pleasure, starting with an afternoon reclining in a bunk with the poppy, followed by an evening of sexual delights, perhaps this time with a small boy.

"Half of your rigging is shot away," the boatyard manager stated as they walked around the war junk. "Were you attacked by pirates?"

Wu nodded innocently, "Yes, the worst kind, on the upper Mekong."

The boatyard manager wasn't fooled, "Yes, I heard they prey on villagers up there. Some day they will meet their fate." He looked Wu in the eyes, until Wu had to look away.

EARLY THE NEXT AFTERNOON, Wu approached the opium den on the waterfront, in an area that looked bombed-out and never repaired. The building seemed to be made of timbers that had washed ashore. The procurer, also the caretaker of the den, was shifty-eyed, nervous, and had the features of a ferret. The caretaker's job was to look out for the opium den's patrons while they were "visiting the poppy" and semi-comatose. Wu wondered about his vulnerability with this man that could be paid to do anything — but his love of the drug, and lust for the very young, drove him on.

"You're early," the caretaker said.

"Well," Wu said, "We have plans for later this evening, right?" and handed him a roll of bills.

The caretaker/procurer was mollified, and said, "Yes, your party is planned." He invited Wu in.

Wu lay back in the bunk and reached for the offered pipe. He took a deep drag and started his visit to Lotus-land, indulging in his fantasies.

Wu never noticed the white-haired coolie moving to the next bunk, or the opium caretaker leaving the room with yet another roll of bills in his hand. Enhanced by the opium, Wu enjoyed almost total recall of the decadent episodes depicted in the polaroids in his cabin. He drew on his pipe, smiling at the memories.

Wu suddenly felt ice drawn across his throat. Gasping, he looked up into the steely eyes of the coolie with white hair, who he recognized as the Yankee from the Mekong.

"What woke you up, Wu, is that I just cut your throat." Ray snarled. "Do you remember Chang Ti and my other friends you murdered in the long tail? Do you remember this knife we played poker for, when you tried to take Lotu?" Ray shouted as he watched Wu bleed out over the side of the bunk.

Then Ray went down, felled by a blow behind his right ear, and crumpled to the floor with Wu's blood dripping on his face. His last thoughts were *"I'm next."*

WHEN RAY REGAINED CONSCIOUSNESS, he lay on a pile of fish nets at the back of a trawler. Next to him was Wu's body, and the opium caretaker. Wu was stripped naked. Ray and the caretaker each had chains knotted around an ankle. Ray could see they were somewhere in the Malacca Strait. The caretaker was awake, bowing and whining in very fast Chinese to a man standing over him. The man wore the disheveled dress of a fisherman, but somehow looked different. Was he a Hmong, the mountain people Ray had heard about? A similar looking man joined him, and they unceremoniously picked up the naked and chained body of Wu and tossed him into the sea.

Ray watched Wu sink below the surface and thought, *"They are cleaning house. No witnesses, no evidence, no reprisals from Wu's people."* He started shaking in terror.

The duo pulled the caretaker to his feet, pushed him to the transom, and motioned him to strip off his clothes. The caretaker cried and kicked at the chain on his ankle. One of the men stepped forward and pulled off the caretakers' clothes, using a knife. The caretaker wailed and wrung his hands, begging for his life in rapid Chinese. The second man casually raised a .45 automatic and shot the caretaker in the forehead, knocking him over the transom into the water.

The trawler was moving at fishing speed, four knots, and Ray saw the body sink in a plume of red. He saw a shark fin glide by. Throwing up, Ray was embarrassed. *"Why am I embarrassed?"* he thought, *"They're going to kill me!"*

RAY THOUGHT OF GISELLE, Miss Teel, RD, his family, *"Hell, it's been a good run. I'll try to die with dignity."* He got up, dragging the chain, to stand at the transom, but he couldn't stop trembling. He stood, legs apart, facing his executioners. One man covered him with his pistol, while the other stepped forward and looked Ray in the face as he tugged at Ray's shirt. Suddenly, as he cut away the shirt, the man's eyes widened, like he just remembered something. He stopped pulling the shirt, and spoke rapidly to the other man, who lowered his gun. They gently took the chain off his ankle and helped Ray back to the pile of nets, indicating he should lay down. Ray couldn't stop shaking. He felt as if the tigers were almost on him.

The boat changed course and picked up speed. A crewman brought him water and helped him move to a small aft cabin. After a while, a crewman in a dirty apron brought him a bowl of noodles and a spicy alcoholic drink. Ray lay back in the bunk and tried to figure out what was happening. *"What did the guy remember, when he looked at me?"* Ray shook his head. *"Where are they taking me now? Are they going to trade me to Wu's people?"* He listened to the boat rushing through the water with a powerful muffled engine. *"This is no ordinary fishing boat. Is it a blockade runner? A smugglers boat?"* Ray felt himself sinking lower and lower into the bunk. *"That spicy drink, did they poison me? No — they just saved me, didn't they? I'm confused,"* he thought, as he sank into a deep sleep.

RAY DIDN'T KNOW HOW long he'd slept when he was awakened, given back his belt knife, and urged forward to the port rail of the boat. Ray stumbled along, still half asleep, and was amazed to see they were tied to his junk in the Hole-in-the-Wall anchorage. They'd brought him home.

As Ray stepped over the rail to his junk, the man that had almost executed him patted him on the shoulder, as if to reassure him all was okay. As the big, muffled trawler quietly left the anchorage, Ray collapsed into his bunk and cried himself to sleep, like a jilted love-struck teenager. He was not ashamed. He slept through the next day, got up and ate, took a shower, then went back to bed and slept some more.

Finally, back on his feet, Ray hit the shower again, as if trying to wash away recent memories. The events were very confusing. As he was getting dressed, still trying to figure out what had happened, the penny dropped.

"I have to go see Lotu."

Ray cabbed to the Presbyterian school on the outskirts of Kuah. Lotu was in class, so Ray waited in the lobby, his back against the wall. After class, Lotu breezed into the lobby, beaming when she saw him.

"Mu-phy!" she ran to him for a hug.

Then she shyly asked, "Mu-phy, is it okay if I call you "Uncle Mu-phy"? The other girls have many uncles close by, and now I only have Uncle Max. Would you be my uncle, too?"

Ray was touched. "I'd be honored to be your uncle, Lotu. Let me take you out to dinner, but first I have a question. Do you wear a moonstone around your neck?"

Lotu smiled. "Why yes, Uncle Mu-phy. It looks just like yours. Daddy has me wear it always, for good luck and protection."

Ray nodded. "For protection?"

"Yes. Daddy put the word out that the wearer of the moonstone has his protection."

Ray smiled and thought, *"The killer on the trawler hadn't remembered something — he'd seen the moonstone as he stripped my shirt."*

Once again, Chow Chee had saved his life.

Ray and Lotu had a good dinner. Later, Ray decided to tell her that she didn't have to worry about Wu Song anymore.

ON THE WAY BACK TO his junk, Ray thought about the tangled web he'd stepped into. The breadth of Chow Chee's reach was amazing. How did he have such influence on the drug runners that ran the opium den? What was their obligation to Chow, that they honored the moonstones? Why were they so intent to erase evidence of Wu's demise? How did they know where my boat was? Ray thought maybe he would never know the answers, but he felt fortunate to be alive.

Chapter 19
The Spice Islands, at Last

Ray approached Max, "Is there another boatyard where we can get repairs? I'm not in the mood for Thailand right now."

Max laughed, "Yes. Penang Island, just down the road, has a good yard, but, let me tell you, the nightlife is not as lively."

Ray smiled, "I've had enough excitement for a while."

The Penang boatyard did a good job, and contrary to predictions, Ray found a bar he liked in Georgetown, the Hong Kong Bar, which was full of characters, and memorabilia from servicemen from around the world. His letters to Giselle, Miss Teel and RD were filled with the wonders of southeast Asia, but did not mention the recent bloody excursions.

He and Max also received news from Chow Chee. Altan and Minoru had made it back safely, which Chee appreciated, as his crew had suffered some losses in the battle against Wu Song's junks. They were now close to full strength, but missing Lotu.

After a period of rest and relaxation, Max and Ray began preparing for their much-anticipated trip to the Spice Islands. They planned to sail Ray's ordinary, undistinguishable junk. They provisioned the boat, got Indonesian visas, and secured charts. The 2500-mile trip would take them down the Malacca Strait, past Singapore, and across the Banda Sea to the Maluku (Spice) Islands.

They would first visit Ambon Island in the Maluku's to see the dark-leaved evergreen tree that grew nutmeg and mace. At an average speed of four knots, the cruising time was estimated at twenty-six days, not counting stops. They would reprovision and refuel at Singapore and Jakarta.

RAY WENT TO SEE LOTU. He felt better about leaving her, with Wu Song no longer a threat.

"Lotu! How are you doing? Will you be okay if Max and I are gone for a few months?"

Lotu smiled, "Don't worry about me, Uncle Mu-phy. School is easy — except for some strict teachers. And I'm getting into politics."

Ray was astounded. Wasn't she only six years old? "Politics?" he asked, dumbly.

"Yes," Lotu answered primly. "I've been elected class president, on a promise to get the school to relax the dress code. They make us wear these ugly dresses that look like choir robes, and we can't even play in them. Even the older girls in school are supporting me."

Ray leaned forward and looked at his shoes, like bowing to a superior force. *"God help us when she's seventeen,"* he thought.

THE CREW OF THE WATER Dog departed Langkawi, bound for the Spice Islands, in great spirits. The boat was heavily loaded for the long voyage. Experience had taught Ray that food and alcohol disappeared quickly. They also carried trade goods for barter with the locals. Fair winds and following seas favored them on the first leg to Singapore, where they took on fuel and water and visited again with Dahl, the Sentosa island development manager.

"Did they find the missing couple?" Ray asked, looking at the abandoned boat.

"Ah, no, and we've lost two more lately, vanished with no trace," Dahl answered. "The police are confused and talk to everybody, but find no one."

Ray said to Max, "Lots of people are being snatched. What do you think is happening?"

A shadow came over Max's face. With the history of persecution in his family, he knew more than he wanted to know. His voice was sad when he spoke. "There is no limit to cruelty, Ray. People are probably being grabbed for some unimaginable purpose, used up, and then discarded, like an old oil filter."

Ray shook his head. "Like we've said, there's a lot of evil out there. Let's be careful."

WHILE IN SINGAPORE, they rode the rapid transit, lost money in a casino, and had a great time in an Irish Bar. On the morning of the third day, Water Dog departed Singapore for Jakarta, on the island of Java, a twelve-day voyage. They sailed down the middle of the Malacca Strait, watching the mangroves for pirates, and anchoring near villages for safety each night. Still in Muslim country, beautiful mosques could be seen and the call to prayer heard as they cruised past even the most rural Indonesian Islands. They approached the bright city of Jakarta at dawn on the eleventh day, dodging the Java ferries, full of commuters from Sumatra.

In Jakarta, Max arranged to meet with yet another business partner, his sixth business. The new venture was in powdered soaps and cleansers, with Max's staff adding water, bottling and labeling the product for sale. Max's search for a chemist had turned up Bulot (which meant "round" in Malaysian), a chubby, world-class chemist who dressed like a boatyard bum. Max was excited about the chemical formulations and predicted success.

Ray harassed him, "Six companies. Geez, Max, when will you get enough?"

Max's answer was very serious. "My father survived on dog's milk in China, and kept goldfish, which represent prosperity and good luck, and colorful Koi, or carp. He told us we could eat them if necessary. His fear of going hungry carried over, I guess. I don't want to ever go hungry."

In a subdued voice, Ray changed the subject. "So, Bulot's brother is a policeman, you said? I thought I heard you two talking about him."

"Yes, Bulot said the police are frustrated because of all the missing people throughout southeast Asia. There are more missing here. He warned us to be careful."

"Man, I'm glad Lotu's safe in that school," Ray said.

While adding to their provisions, Ray explored Jakarta's spice shops in search of the local popular spice called bumbu, a stone-ground blend of peppers, garlic, ginger, lemongrass and other spices. He was delighted with his find, and added it to his spice inventory. Max was the taste tester for the dish of Bumbu Clams; and gave his stamp of approval.

Heading east, they stopped at more islands, and Ray marveled at the sights. Live volcanoes hovered over lush tropical growth, villages with colorful fishing boats, horse-drawn carts, massive wooden freighters being built on the beach with hand tools, more ornate mosques and lots of friendly, happy people. The passage across the Java Sea was uneventful, with the exception of an hour in the evenings, when Max taught himself to play the ukulele he'd purchased in Jakarta. The sound was awful and when Ray could stand it no longer, he sent Max to the foredeck to practice. It wasn't far enough.

FINALLY, THEY APPROACHED the Maluku Spice Island chain, and altered course for the island of Ambon, home of the spices they'd come to see. It was midnight, with a gentle breeze, and Water Dog glided softly toward the island. Ray was excited. This was the culmination of his and Giselle's dream. He could see the outline of Ambon in the distance. A remote shadow of another island was off to the left.

"That must be Buru Island, where the prison was, until it closed in 1980," Max said. They'd done their research.

"Mostly political prisoners, wasn't it?" Ray asked.

"Yeah, mostly communists, they really came down on them," Max said. "Is that a fire over there?"

"Yeah. Let's steer over that way and take a look." Ray said.

As they got closer to Buru, they could barely hear excited voices in the quiet night air, then nothing, and the fire, which seemed to be just offshore of the island, abruptly went out, and all went silent. It was puzzling, but they were excited about Ambon, so they continued on their way.

At dawn, they made landfall in Ambon, dinghied ashore and at last walked among trees that bore the treasured nutmeg and mace. The trees were beautiful, with the dark brown nutmeg nuts with their "caps" of bright red mace. Ray was excited but sad at the same time. He imagined what it might have been like to be here with Giselle, picking the nuts, examining and discussing how it became the most sought-after spice throughout the world, starting in the year 1650.

Max and Ray ventured down a road to a small village, past a plant that processed nutmeg. In the village, they met the owner, who was also the village mayor. He knew all about the history of nutmeg in Indonesia, and took them for a tour of the plant. Ray and Max were amazed at the operation, with picking and cleaning rooms, conveyor belts to vibrating screens for sorting grading and packing. It seemed a huge operation for such a small island, as they processed the spices for several surrounding islands.

They toured the island for three days, looking at other spices growing and their processing operations, meeting local farmers, and taking in the sights. The growers of other spices had similar arrangements for processing spices grown on neighboring islands in warehouses in Ambon. Max had an easy rapport, and the people they met were friendly, generous, and anxious to gain a new customers.

Max and Ray had a grand time and finally headed back to the beach and the anchored Water Dog. They built a fire on the beach, ate coconut meat and drank arak. It was a well-deserved celebration, and immensely satisfying. With hammocks strung between the coconut trees, they took naps and discussed the voyage home.

They departed Ambon the next morning with sacks full of nutmeg nuts, vanilla beans, and various other spices. Max also had lists of contacts on the other spice islands and several trade agreements to supply spices to his trading company.

AS THEY PASSED BURU Island, Ray's curiosity kicked in. "What say we cruise by the beach where we saw that fire?"

They entered the small bay and noticed ashes along the beach at the waterline. "Looks like something burned in the water," Max said.

They scanned the beach with binoculars, and saw many footprints in the sand, all headed inland. There was movement in the brush.

"Rats!" Ray shouted. "Look at those big white spotted rats, lots of them!"

Max looked and started shaking his head. "Oh my. I've seen that kind of rat before — but I can't believe it."

"What?" Ray asked.

"Those are Sri Lankan rats. I've been all over southeast Asia, and I've seen them in Sri Lanka, big and white, with spots."

"So, how'd they get here?" Ray asked.

"Well, they come off boats, but why are they here?"

They let the junk drift in closer to shore, while wondering about the rats. Suddenly, through the brush, a man came running toward them, at full speed, arms waving. He ran straight into the water, arms still waving, trying to swim at the same time.

He was hollering, in English, "Help me please, help me! We must get my wife, she's back there."

Max heard a splash. Ray had dropped the anchor and was lowering the dinghy. The man was wearing ragged clothes and was emaciated. He was hysterical as they pulled him aboard the dinghy.

"Please go get her before the dragons do, they will kill her!"

Ray looked at Max, "Dragons? There are dragons in Indonesia?"

Max nodded, "Yes, but not here; they're way over on Komodo Island. Komodo dragons, giant lizards that can kill a water buffalo. Anything it bites is poisoned by its saliva."

Ray looked at the heavens, as if imploring God, "Tigers, river pirates, sharks, and now poison dragons?"

"Yes, yes, yes!" the man said, frantically. "The dragons are here, and will kill her! I saw your boat, it's our only chance."

They rowed the dinghy to the beach and followed the man's tracks inland.

The man followed, "Her name is Gale Fisher, I'm Andy." He called out, "Gale! We're coming!"

They reached the tree where Andy thought she'd been hiding, but she wasn't there. They heard grunting and thrashing in the brush. Andy collapsed in the fetal position, shaking all over.

He cried, "Oh no! It got her, the dragon got her!"

The noises got closer, and two Komodo dragons burst through the brush, almost on top of them. The lizard's wide mouths were open and snapping, low heads swinging back and forth, short powerful legs lifting their thick bodies clear of the sand. Long, dripping tongues shot out past yellow teeth.

THERE WAS NOWHERE TO go, so they ran back to the dinghy. Ray felt the horror of the tigers just behind him again. Back on the boat, they tried to calm Andy down.

"What the hell's going on?" asked Max.

Ray brought Andy water, and they waited for an explanation. Andy drank, nodding in appreciation, and started talking.

"Gale and I were snatched off the street in Singapore, stuffed into a panel van, and brought here in the hold of a ship. There were others with us."

He drank more water and Ray tried to get him to eat some noodles, but he broke down, crying again. "I can't believe she's gone!"

Ray gave him a shot of arak to calm him.

"That monster, the big Dutchman, has people processing nutmeg and other plants and spices into various chemicals and adding stuff to make designer drugs. The process is labor intensive, and the substances are toxic when handled too much, causing tremors. The Dutchman just eliminates the sick workers and gets more. He gets rid of most of the bodies in acid baths in the other old prison building. But they leave some bodies out for the dragons. The dragons are like guards. It's horrible!"

Andy was crying while he told them, "They learned that an early sign of tremors is a blackening tongue. They'd check our tongues every morning, to decide if we would die." He rocked back and forth, holding his stomach. "Some people last longer than others, but the Dutchman needs lots of people. He's bringing in Sri Lankan refugee boats, sets them on fire in the bay to sink them. Those that can't work go to the baths."

Max cleaned his glasses, "That explains the ashes on the beach and the spotted rats."

Ray tilted his head, "How do you know all this, Andy?"

Andy drank more arak. "They're using almost all the rooms in the old prison. I ended up in the guard tower, where I could see and hear almost everything. The acid baths give me nightmares. The Dutchman lines up the sick ones by the tank and shoots them." He started wailing at the thought. "As they are selected to die, they pray the shots will kill them before they hit the acid." Andy wrung his hands. "Would you please go find Gale? I can't bear the thought of her being out there. She might be suffering, not dead yet."

Max looked up to see Ray putting on his vest with the .45. He handed Max a full pack as he asked, "How big do these motherfucking dragons get? Do you think there are more?"

Max took the pack which held water bottles, binoculars and machetes. "They run up to about ten feet and three hundred pounds, and they're fast."

"Holy shit. I'm scared already. Let's leave Andy here and see if we can find Gale."

BACK ASHORE, THEY FOLLOWED the trail inland again, with Ray up front with the .45 and a machete.

"Max, I wish I could hit something besides the side of a barn with this pistol, much less a big fast lizard."

"I've never shot one. Maybe we should rely on stealth," Max said.

They saw no signs of Gale as they worked around for a view of the prison courtyard, climbed a tree, sat and watched, and worried about the Komodo dragons.

"Did you ask Andy how they escaped?" Ray asked Max.

"Yeah. It was luck. He said they were simply overlooked as people were being shuffled back and forth. He said the Dutchmen rely on the lizards a lot for security, they brought them over from Komodo on one of their slave runs."

"How do you transport a dragon?" Ray asked.

"Andy said they use their own dope."

Two hours later, a big, tattooed Dutchman came out to work in the prison courtyard garden.

Max chuckled. "Seems unreal, a drug dealer/heartless killer like that picking tomatoes in his garden."

But Ray was entranced, looking through his binoculars at the Dutchman. "Max, you ain't gonna believe this, but I stuck a fork in that guy's belly up in China, a while back."

Max looked at Ray in disbelief. Ray told him the story.

"People were missing up there too, maybe he was recruiting for his workforce." Ray said.

They felt a bump on the tree below, and saw a huge Komodo dragon looking up at them.

Max, below Ray in the tree, said, "Ray, could you climb a little higher, please?"

As he climbed, Ray said, "What the hell do we do now?"

"Maybe we should sit very still," said Max.

They watched the big lizard looking up at them. It's yellow eyes had a vacant, hooded look, sort of like a crocodile.

"What are we going to do?" Max asked. "What's that sound?"

They sat quietly and listened. They could hear the dragon's breathing, and a hacking sound came through the trees, sounding almost like laughing. Looking closely, they saw a woman in another tree, twenty yards away, almost hidden. She was looking at them, laughing with a wild look, her side and thigh bleeding. She rocked back and forth, her mouth working without saying anything.

She laughed again, "The beast has killed me, but I'm not dead yet."

Ray asked Max, "Has she gone mad?"

"Looks like it. What can we do?"

They watched her for thirty minutes, with the dragon trapping them from below, rubbing against the tree, as if in anticipation. A bell started ringing in the courtyard. To their amazement, the dragon lurched toward the sound.

"Must be feeding time," Ray said.

Max was already scrambling down the tree. "Let's get the mad lady and haul out of here," he said, over his shoulder.

They had to coax her out of the tree. It was as if she didn't believe they were real.

"Gale, Andy's waiting on the boat, come on down!" Max said.

Ray was looking around, worried about guards and lizards. She finally came down and they hustled her toward the beach. She kept rolling her head around.

"It don't matter, I'm bit, and I'm dead."

They helped Gale into the dinghy and rowed to the junk. She didn't recognize Andy and kept laughing and shaking her head.

"We need to get her to Ambon, to a doctor," Max said.

She had lacerations across her side and thigh, that looked infected already.

As Ray pulled anchor, he said "The mayor in Ambon can find a doctor and the police, for the lash-up back there."

Max said, "Lash-up?"

AMBON VILLAGE HAD A doctor, and the police were very interested in the story Andy had to tell. Arrangements were made to raid the old prison the next day. Gale and Andy were transported to the hospital in Kota for treatment of the infection.

Ray and Max sailed back to Buru Island, to see how the raid went. They ghosted into the same bay, and with the shallow draft of the junk and favorable tides, were able to touch shore and put a ramp down to the beach. They arrived well after the raid, but still heard yelling and gunfire. They'd been advised by the police to not go ashore until given clearance. So Max and Ray sat in the junk, drinking arak and speculating.

"How many poor souls are in there, you think?"

"Andy said more than a hundred. Amazing, isn't it?"

"Yeah, hope they catch the fat Dutchman."

Soon, they looked out to see the police chief coming up the ramp. He was excited.

"Good news, men. The druggies are locked in a cell here, for now, and we've ordered a ferry to pick up the captives here on the beach. They are heading this way, — I told them of your role in all this, and they want to thank you."

"Chief, did you catch the big Dutchman?"

He shook his head, with a funny look on his face. "No. In the excitement, we thought we had lost him. But the captives shoved him into the acid bath — alive. And, you know what? I didn't see a thing."

They sat with the police chief on the fantail, drinking arak as they waited for the freed hostages. Almost a hundred captives, close together, helping each other, approached the beach, cheering and waving. They cheered and cheered, with amazing enthusiasm for people as weak and sick as they were.

"How does it feel to be heroes?" the chief said.

Ray and Max were overcome with emotion, looking at the haggard souls paying respect to them, giving it all they had.

Suddenly, Ray found himself walking down the ramp to meet Giselle, standing in front of the crowd. She looked torn and ragged, but the same — the saucy way she stood, red hair cascading down her front, fair skin, green eyes, bent St. Christophers medal — he walked to her, smiling. It was unbelievable.

"Giselle!" he called. "How can it be?"

She smiled back, and stepped into his arms as she said, "I'm Stella, Giselle's sister. I read all your letters to Paris, and I had to come."

Epilog

Ray & Stella now live on a long boat in Paris, and manage the "Facing Heaven Spice Company," named for the taijin pepper, in honor of Chang Ti, Ray's friend from the River Dragon, killed by Wu Song. Maxmillian Chee is a partner in the business, operating out of Malaysia. General Sabo arranged for Ray and Stella's wedding at the Notre Dame Cathedral. The three hundred guests included Miss Teel and RD Carrera, Clink Parker, Maxmillian Chee and Lotu.

On her many visits, Miss Teel cruises the national library of France, called the Bibliothèque Nationale de France, and the Louvre Museum. Ray and Stella spoil her with lavish accommodation when she visits. Miss Teel travels on the income from her bestseller, "Travels of the Spice Hound" which was compiled from the letters Ray had written on his travels.

RD Carrera also visits Ray and Stella when he's taking a break from his thriving bar business. He has toured all the castles of France and really enjoys the cabarets on the Left Bank. RD doesn't think about Alice Parker anymore, as he has found good company in both France and Odessa.

Clink Parker is still aboard the M/V Irony, enjoying his travels and trading. His sister hasn't moved again, much to his delight.

Chow Chee, Minoru and Altan are still on the Mekong. Each of them has a large, beautiful war junk, though not much pirating is done anymore. Minoru married one of Chow's sisters, and they have six kids. Altan has two wives, both live ashore.

Lotu graduated early from Malaysian high school, and is attending Le Cordon Bleu in Paris to become a chef. Like Giselle, she has grand plans to start a world-class restaurant. Ray is considering partnering with her in this venture.

The End

Acknowledgements

A large part of this story takes place in Southeast Asia. While cruising, we spent quite some time there, doing boat work and visiting Indonesia, Malaysia and Thailand. When you make landfall in a cruising boat, you are dealing with working people on the waterfront; at the marinas, rigging and welding shops, and storefront kiosks serving the cruising community. The cruising community consists of all types of sailors from around the globe, interfacing with locals of all ethnicities and faiths. Many of the people we met along the way show up as characters in this book.

What was amazing, with all those cultures, languages and ethnic groups, and varying Islamic, Hindu, Buddhist, Christian and other faiths, was that everyone seemed to get along, recognizing their differences and accommodating each other. We hope this story acknowledges this admirable trait and encourages us all to live together in harmony.

Don't miss out!

Visit the website below and you can sign up to receive emails whenever Jerry Reid publishes a new book. There's no charge and no obligation.

https://books2read.com/r/B-A-TTMN-RBAXC

BOOKS 2 READ

Connecting independent readers to independent writers.

Did you love *The Spice Hound's Adventures*? Then you should read *Hunter's Eyes*[1] by Jerry Reid!

From a young age, Trosclair dreamed of having a plantation-style house on the high ground west of Iberia, where he could sight his rifle on the fence line, sit on the porch with the love of his life, and listen to the mockingbirds. When the war came, his skills from the oil fields, shrimp boats, moonshine stills and poaching served him well. Trosclair found himself in the United States Marine Corps, leading a Force Recon team in Vietnam. The loss of two team members leads Trosclair to revenge, where he nearly loses his life, but instead finds love and riches. Returning home, he finds his

---

1. https://books2read.com/u/3n20rK

2. https://books2read.com/u/3n20rK

land in Louisiana and shares his wealth with the friends from the battlefields. He has Mae Lee, the light of his life and kindred spirit, and the future looks bright. On the eve of their wedding day, while fishing for shrimp for the reception, a breaking wave over the transom caused the boat to broach. Trosclair regained consciousness to find Mae Lee missing. She was gone. Trosclair survived but was devastated by the loss, and disappears. As months go by, strange incidents occur which cause friends and family to think Mae Lee may be alive, and has been taken for a reason. Trosclair must be found. The search for Trosclair and Mae Lee is on, from faraway Alaska, to the San Juan Islands of the Pacific Northwest, to Panama. Trosclair and his friends take on old enemies, forge new alliances, and go farther than they thought possible.

Also by Jerry Reid

Hunter's Eyes
Escape from Mongolia
Madison Teagarden's Quest
The Spice Hound's Adventures

About the Author

Jerry Reid's passion is exploring inland waterways, bays and estuaries in his 32-foot shallow-draft sloop, observing wildlife in quiet anchorages while eating good food, drinking box wine, and reading good books with his first mate Joni. He sails out of Bellingham, Washington.

Jerry's comments: Thank you for looking at this book. The characters in my stories are largely drawn from my experiences, ranging from digging ditches in Texas, a hitch in the Marine Corps, flying charter in the mountains of the Pacific Northwest, building a 40-foot sailboat in my backyard, to sailing on a 10-year circumnavigation and visiting 40 countries. The characters also come from friends, relatives and acquaintances — so look for yourself, you may be in this book.

The appeal to me of writing adventure stories is the opportunity to join with these characters, some far away or no longer with us — to enjoy their company once more in my memories, and see what they do this time. Stay safe in these times, and enjoy life. - Jerry

About the Publisher

Oxbow Publishing prints adventure stories and character-driven tales. If you have comments on this book or other Oxbow Publishing books, you can reach us at oxbowcompany@gmail.com.

Oxbow Publishing has made possible these books by Jerry Reid:

Hunter's Eyes

Escape from Mongolia

Madison Teagarden's Quest: Pursuit of a Madman on Vanuatu.

The Spice Hound's Adventures

www.ingramcontent.com/pod-product-compliance
Lightning Source LLC
Chambersburg PA
CBHW031130130726
47988CB00006B/2313